Bootleg Shirt

A Novel by Mary Denomie

Bootleg Shirt

DEDICATION

I honestly never thought this book would be published. I originally wrote it in the mid-90s. As a setting, I used a bootleg t-shirt company where I worked in the mid-80s. That was where I picked up my knowledge of the business, such as it is. All characters and events in the book are completely fictitious, however.

I attempted to publish the book in the late 90s without success. At some point I managed to lose the entire book— all three formats. I had often thought of starting over, but it seemed too daunting since I had a family and a career taking up my time.

In February of 2022, my friend since grade school— Pam Daniel – discovered a complete copy of Bootleg Shirt she had on her bookshelf for 20 years without realizing it. I was thrilled, and I continue to be grateful to Pam for making this happen. Pam, you are awesome.

I must also thank Pam for introducing me to the ladies at Crystal Heart Imprints, a cooperative publishing association. My experience with trying to get a literary agent when I first wrote this book, convinced me I did not want to go querying this time around.

I would like to thank my Dad, Bob Korbas, for his excellent proofreading skills. He also assured I would keep working by texting, "When will I get the next chapter?" He really kept me moving forward. Pops, you are an excellent editor and coach! I can't thank you enough.

CHAPTER 1

MONDAY, JANUARY 25, 1988

The streetlights were still on as June left her apartment on Monday morning. It was snowing hard, and she was grateful her old Chevette was parked on the next block. It was the first heavy snow of the winter. Thundersnow rumbling, echoing off the old brick warehouse at the center of June's neighborhood, and bouncing off the slat-sided double-flats lining the other side of the street, as June trudged through 4 inches of sticky accumulation.

Why couldn't it have been a foot? she thought to herself. In Wisconsin, it had to snow at least that much before they canceled anything. Four inches was just a pain in the ass for everybody. June hated driving her old heap in the snow. The tires were practically bald, and she slid into spots rather than stopping on them.

The car started on the first try. June rolled her eyes. "Stupid piece of junk!" She got the shovel out of the back at the same time filling her hatch with snow that slid down the door as soon as she lifted it. She swore and slammed the hatch closed.

She had to hurry and dig out her car or she would be late to her interview. There was no way she was going to let that happen. Probably. She did a half-assed job clearing her windows and almost pulled out right in front of a passing plow. It laid on its horn and plowed a giant ridge of snow behind June's rear tires. She tried gunning the Chevette to try to get over the pile, but after way too many attempts, she had to get out and shovel the back clear a second time.

The ride downtown was a nightmare for the under-insured. The bald tires and mushy brakes were impossible on slush. June had the world's slowest accident as she very, very slowly rear-ended a cab at a redlight on Wisconsin Avenue. It was almost silly. June would have laughed, but the cab driver jumped out of his cab and screamed at her for a full minute before looking at his undamaged bumper and then driving away. It left her shaken, and she started to feel like maybe this wasn't going to turn out the way she had hoped.

The day before, June had scanned the Sunday Sentinel want ads. Her biggest problem was not being sure what kind of job to look for. They all sounded boring: telemarketing, office work, retail sales, or God-forbid, waiting tables. Since she had moved down to Milwaukee 18 months ago, June had been unemployed three times. This made four. She was never without a job for long; she had to eat.

June knew her employment record looked terrible on her resumé, but all her jobs had been so dull they felt like a form of nonsurgical frontal lobotomy. The work was tedious, the people she worked with even more so, and the prospects were nonexistent.

She just couldn't stand it anymore. Somewhere there was a job that she could handle for longer than six months without going mad. But suddenly she saw an ad she hadn't seen many times before. It said, "NEEDED: Sales Manager for a T-shirt Company." No other information given, apart from a phone number. Normally she wouldn't bother with such a vague ad, but she decided she needed to take a few chances if she was going to get out of her rut.

She called and the phone was answered promptly by a woman, "Rock Shirts!"

"Hi! I'm calling about your ad in the Sunday paper for a sales manager."

"Do you have a resumé?"

"Yes."

"Can you come in for an interview?"

"Sure." June was given an address near the river. "When would you like me to be there?"

"How fast can you get here?"

June considered the accumulating snow. "An hour?"

"Okay but hurry up. See if you can get here faster. Everyone is late because of the snow. Just come up to the 3rd floor." June wondered if this was a test.

June pulled into a space along a derelict warehouse right on the Milwaukee River. June opened the squeaky door on the Chevette and was immediately hit with the aroma of dry dog food. A sign across the river proclaimed BADGERLAND BYPRODUCTS. Charming.

The door was at the corner of the building. There was a very little lobby space, just a spot to stand in while waiting for the elevator. When the doors opened on the 3rd floor, June found herself at one end of a long narrow corridor. There were doors periodically, but none of them had names, or even numbers.

She knocked on the first door to the right, but there was a lot of loud machinery running on the other side of the door. In any event, no one answered her knock. So June pounded a bit louder.

The door was flung open by a skinny girl with an ugly haircut and an irritated expression. She was wearing a black t-shirt for a band called the Brutal Tulips. Behind her there was an enormous machine pinwheeling around. Another girl was pulling the t-shirts off the machine and throwing them onto a conveyor belt feeding into an industrial dryer that ran the length of the huge room. They were moving too fast for her to see what they said on them, but they looked like a heavy metal band black t-shirt.

"Well? Whatcha want?" the girl asked with considerable annoyance.

"I'm here for an interview." June shouted over the din.

The girl wiped her hands on a rag and gave June the once over and June regretted her decision to wear a business suit with a grey bow blouse. She tried her best to appear aloof, actually, she felt a fool. "It's across the hall," she told June. "First door on the left."

"Thanks," June smiled but the girl with the ugly haircut had already spun around and was walking away.

The door across the hall had a frosted glass window, and she could hear someone talking softly on the other side. June knocked politely.

"COME IN," a woman bellowed loudly. June thought it might be the same woman she had spoken to on the phone. She opened the door to find herself in a shabby front office, with huge windows filling one wall. The snowstorm looked beautiful through the tangle of a dozen hanging plants.

A small woman was seated at a large wooden desk in the corner. She was wearing jeans and a t-shirt for a band called Run Around Naked. At least June THOUGHT it was a band. Maybe it was just her motto or something. She looked at June with surprise. *This suit was a REALLY bad idea*, thought June.

"Hi. My name is June Forrest. I'm here for an interview." June handed her resumé to the woman, who continued to look at June with a mixture of amazement and suspicion.

The woman stood up and moved to an ornately carved wooden door that seemed completely out of place in the shabby outer office. "I'll tell Jerry you're here. He's the owner," she said as she rapped lightly on the door. She didn't wait for an answer, instead opening the door and striding in. June could hear a man with a booming voice, apparently on the telephone. She strode right out again and said, "Go on in and have a seat. Jerry will be off the phone in a minute."

June straightened herself and put on her best business smile before she strode into the owner's private office. The inner office was large and had the same wall of windows filled with plants. But it took June a minute to acclimate herself to the furnishings.

The walls were filled with weird artifacts. There were animal skin rugs on the floor and antique furniture in various styles and states of disrepair.

A big man with a beard and an unstylish, ill-fitting suit with an orange paisley tie was sitting at a cluttered desk and talking animatedly into his phone. He could have been several years more or less than fifty, but it was difficult to tell. He waved her toward a moldy looking armchair piled with t-shirts.

June scooped up the shirts and dumped them onto an equally cluttered settee. She sat down carefully onto the wobbly chair.

"You need to order Auntie M and the Cyclones," he was telling someone. "They will fly out of your store for 15 bucks!"

It was at that precise moment that June saw the iguana. It was standing on the edge of the desk directly in front of her, and it was staring her in the face.

June squawked involuntarily and jerked backwards, tipping over the moldy chair and rolling awkwardly onto a mangy bear rug.

Jerry stood up to look at her over his desk. He moved the phone away from his mouth and told her, "It's stuffed," before resuming his phone conversation.

June stood up with her heart pounding. Well, NOW it was obvious the thing was stuffed. It was not in good condition, and its toes were all curled up which made it lean at a strange angle.

He put that there to deliberately freak people out. June thought. *What kind of game is this guy playing? Is this his idea of a corporate power maneuver?* June decided she would refuse to be shocked, no matter what else happened. *Anyway, what else could happen?*

Jerry hung up the phone and then immediately took another call. June thought, *How rude,* but on second thought she was glad for the extra time to regain her composure. He glanced over her resumé while he was listening to the caller. The girl with the ugly haircut appeared at the office door. Finding Jerry on the phone, she looked around for a place to sit. She eventually decided to sit on the floor.

June smiled at her "Hi. I'm June. Thanks for the directions earlier."

"It's okay."

"Uhm, what's your name?" June tried to look friendly.

The girl with the ugly haircut looked her over again. "Peg." She said finally.

See? That didn't hurt, June thought. She gave up on the idea of conversation.

Another woman came into the office. She had a big blond hairdo with black roots and lots of powder blue eyeshadow. She was plump and was stuffed into tight jeans and a tighter sleeveless top.

She groaned when she saw Jerry on the phone and leaned against the doorframe to wait. A minute later a man in ink-stained clothes also tried to enter the office. Seeing the three women, he sighed heavily and leaned against the wall outside the office. Jerry ended his call, and they all rushed up to his desk and began talking at once. Except June, of course. She was practicing being unflappable.

Jerry stood up and walked toward the door while being yelled at by everyone at once. He was tall – a bit over six feet and a bit over 200 pounds, and his employees circled him like noisy satellites circling a planet. Jerry signaled to June over the heads of the others, "Come with me." Two more people waving pieces of paper joined in. "Print the Chain Smoking Alter Boys next," Jerry yelled, and Peg ran off down the hall, satisfied for the present.

Down the hall one of the satellites yelled, "We are still out of The Inflatable Women!"

"Who cares!" Jerry suddenly became annoyed. "They don't sell." He opened a door to the right to reveal several people on the phone. "Stop taking orders for The Inflatable Women." He looked around for June. "This is the phone room," he said for her benefit.

June stepped into a large closet. There were three people with a phone to one ear and a finger shoved in the other ear. *It's Dickensian,* she thought.

"People keep ordering it," someone protested.

"Talk them out of it. They won't sell and they will just send them back. Tell them to order the Chain Smoking Alter Boys instead."

The noisy knot of people moved off through the winding corridors that made up the place. It was like someone just put up walls and doors at random without a plan. *It's a hopeless rat's maze,* June decided. June gave a pinched smile to the phone orphans before closing the door and following Jerry. She found him in a huge room filled with row after row of DIY shelves made from 2X4s and plywood. The shelves were all piled high with t-shirts— thousands of t-shirts. Jerry was finishing his conversation with his last satellite as June caught up with them.

"So, Judy, is it?" he asked.

"That's June."

"Right! Right." He looked her over in a way that made her feel cheap. "You look good. Your resumé looks good. But I think you may be over-qualified for this job. I'm afraid you will find something better and be gone in a week."

June tried not to look incredulous. She had been hired at a couple of decent companies, but she wasn't at either of them very long. "How much does the position pay?" June knew this wasn't a great opening question, but she was starting to wonder if she should bail out immediately.

"That depends on the commission."

"Commission? I thought it was a management job."

"Your commission would be based on the total sales of the sales department."

June thought about the three people in the closet and made a face.

Jerry noticed the expression. "Wait! You haven't seen the best part." He opened another door and gestured for June to enter the very large, very dusty, very empty room. The two end walls were brick. The long wall was made of little panes of filthy glass that let in a greasy light. The floor was wood, but so dirty it looked like packed mud. The room was big enough to need eight large concrete pillars to hold up the floor above.

Jerry walked to the center of the room and swept out his arms as if encompassing a great treasure. "Well? What do you think of THIS?"

June tried not to look completely disappointed. "What is it?"

"THIS is the new phone room!" He hurried over to June with his eyes sparkling. "I am having twenty phones put in here. When we get everything set up, you could wind up making commission on two shifts of twenty people." He rubbed his hands together like a greedy troll.

"You talked me into it. I mean, if I have the job."

"Can you start tomorrow?"

What was June getting herself into? What did she really know about the job? She was pretty sure it wouldn't be boring. "Absolutely." June shook her new boss' hand.

CHAPTER 2

WEDNESDAY, JANUARY 17, 1988

June arrived for work the next morning a little early, and a lot nervous. She found a parking place a few blocks away from the building so nobody would see her getting out of the Shove-It. She was dressed in a new sweatshirt and a comfortable pair of jeans.

She had her hair pulled back in a neat ponytail and she was trying her best to be professional. She navigated through the winding hallways to the front office and found the secretary at her desk.

"Can I help you," the woman said, without looking up.

"Yes, I'm June. I was here yesterday. I'm supposed to start working today."

"Oh. I didn't recognize you without the suit," she said without sarcasm. "I'm Debbie, the office manager. I need you to fill out some forms. Have a seat."

June sat on an ancient velvet sofa that was so saggy, her ass ended up about 6 inches off the floor. Her long legs meant her knees poked up rather awkwardly, so she ended up turning sideways and perching on the front edge of the sofa's frame. She filled out all the usual forms for employment, income tax and social security and all of that. June realized Debbie was staring at her the whole time, smirking.

"The Mona Lisa!" June suddenly realized. "That's who she looks like."

June managed to extract herself from the sofa and she handed Debbie her paperwork with what she hoped was a confident expression.

Debbie took them without looking at them. "The hours are generally 9:30 to 3:30 with a half hour for lunch," she told June.

"That's all? I thought it was full time."

"Oh, that is full time around here. It doesn't make a difference to your paycheck anyway. You will get paid 1% of all sales made by the sales staff. That's everything except the sales Jerry makes himself."

"How much does that usually average?"

"I don't know." Debbie looked at her blankly. "We've never had a sales manager before."

"Well, how much did you have in sales last week?"

"I don't know."

June was getting exasperated. "I need some idea of what I am going to be paid. At least roughly."

"Jerry said that we had to pay you at least $4 an hour."

A knot formed in June's stomach. Minimum wage and only 30 hours a week besides.

"It should work out to be more than that, though."

Debbie tried to assure her. "Jerry wants to show you around himself today. He should be here in a few minutes."

Debbie got up and came around the desk. She handed June a long sheet of paper with tiny print on both sides. "This is our list of shirts. All the band shirts are on the front, and all the dirty expression shirts are on the back.

"You may want to start familiarizing yourself with our stock. You can go down and look in the print room to see what's on the shelves, too. I'll let you know when Jerry gets here." Debbie turned and started to leave the room.

June looked at the list she was given. At the top of the list it said, *Rock Shirts, Inc. – Jack Snow, owner.*

"Who is Jack Snow," June called after Debbie.

Debbie turned around. "That's Jerry. Jack Snow is his alias."

"Why does he need an alias?" June said with alarm.

"Because they are bootleg." Debbie pointed to the list in June's hand. She turned and left the room as June stood there, trying to digest this bit of important information. She looked down at the list again. There were hundreds of shirts for popular bands, cartoon characters, and celebrities.

The other side of the paper had hundreds of rude expressions they would put on a shirt. June was familiar with the genre.

'Life's a Bitch and Then You Die', and other philosophical gems. The price listed was $3 for 100% cotton shirts and $4 for the 50/50 USA made shirts. Of course they are bootleg. They are far too cheap to be licensed. A shirt for a top-selling rock group cost as much as one that said, 'Same Shit, Different Day.'

Even though she tried not to get her hopes up, June was crushed. She was trying to decide if she should just walk out, when Jerry swooped into the office carrying a large shopping bag.

"Come on, everybody," he yelled in his booming voice. "I got us all pastries from La Bourgeoisie."

June laughed at his intentional mispronunciation. La Boulangerie was a nearby French restaurant and bakery.

"Hey, you showed up," Jerry said to June with surprise. "I'm glad somebody gets that joke."

About 15 people had come out of every nook and cranny of the rat's maze, as Jerry boisterously handed out croissants.

"Help yourselves," he told everyone while happily munching on one. "I have an announcement," Jerry bellowed. "This is June. She's our new sales manager. She will be helping me interview people for the next several days, but after that, you will be seeing a lot of her around here."

June wished she had done a runner when she had the chance. "Hi, everybody." She waved to the group. The majority were quite young, but it was a diverse group that gathered around for breakfast.

"Jerry, you must have stopped in the print room before you came in here this morning," Debbie said with a smirk.

"Yes, to invite them to breakfast. How did you know," he asked her.

"You've got ink all over the back of your suit."

A large multicolored streak of ink crossed the back side of the jacket and trousers of a different but equally unstylish suit, much to the amusement of the crowd.

June watched the group with interest. Jerry Cooper might be a crook, but he seemed to like his employees, and they genuinely seemed to like him.

"Come into the office." Jerry headed through the carved door.

June grabbed a bun and a cup of coffee and followed him. "Um, Mr. Cooper," June began.

"Please, PLEASE, call me Jerry, for heaven's sake. How's the croissant?" Jerry was piling old t-shirts on his chair so that he could sit down without getting ink everywhere. After fiddling for a while, he plunked down and sighed. He smiled at June, and she couldn't help but notice that he had an awful lot of crumbs in his beard.

"Okay, fine," she managed to stammer. "Look, Jerry..." she began again.

"You're having second thoughts, aren't you?"

"You never mentioned that what you are doing is illegal."

"It's not," he insisted. "I've had a lawyer look into everything. Let me give you the tour and explain a few things before you decide."

June had never had anyone try to talk her into taking a job before. She decided to hear him out. After all, she could always turn them all in for a reward if things don't work out. She might as well leave all her options open.

"Okay, convince me." June sighed and sat down in the wobbly chair.

"First of all, if someone asks, 'Why are these shirts so cheap?' we say, 'Because they are bootleg,' so it's not fraud. Just copyright infringement."

"Isn't that illegal too?"

"Yes, but not AS illegal. I can't be sent to jail. They can only sue me. I mean, we have our own artist, and she creates all our own designs. Come with me," he said, jumping up and heading out the door, dragging an old t-shirt stuck to the ink on the seat of his pants.

June had to jump up and hurry after him. He led her to one of the many hidden offices that made up the rat's maze. Inside was a room dominated by a huge artist's easel with a built-in light table for viewing transparencies.

Jerry introduced the woman working inside. "June, I'd like you to meet our artist, Terri."

"How do you do?" June shook Terri's dainty hand. *An artist's hand*, June thought. She was slim, and conservatively dressed in a skirt and sweater. She seemed kind of shy, and June wondered how Jerry had convinced her to work for him. In a sudden fit of boldness, June decided to ask her. "Do you like your job here?"

Terri laughed and glanced at Jerry, who just shrugged.

"Yes, very much. Jerry's a good boss," she chuckled.

Terri looked about 40, but she wore heavy make-up to cover a bad complexion, so it was difficult to guess. The traces of teenage acne could be the cause of her shyness. Several examples of her work hung on the walls of the little office. June had to admit, she was very impressed. Jerry must blow all the overhead on his artist. Terri had obvious talent.

"Come on," Jerry looked at June. "Lots to see."

June was suddenly reminded of Willy Wonka.

"She you later." June smiled at Terri as she hurried to catch up with her boss. She found him in the print room.

"Jerry, you have a t-shirt stuck to your ass," Peg's voice came from the top of one of the presses. Today her hair was purple and spiked straight up. June thought it looked worse. Peg was installing a large wooden frame onto the printer. It looked a lot like an artist's canvas. It had backward lettering on it, and June realized it must be a silk screen.

"Gross," Peg yelled. "Your beard's full of food, too."

Jerry removed the t-shirt and used it to wipe his face before flinging it under the press. June was surprised he didn't get any ink on his face.

Without missing a beat, Jerry boomed, "This is the print room. We have two machines, although only one is presently working." He thumped the side of the idle one with his fist, and June jumped with surprise when a groan came from within the machinery.

A greasy dirty Popeye the Sailor stuck his head out from under the press. "Don't bang when I'm working."

"When will this press work," Jerry said too loudly.

"When hell freezes over," Popeye said louder.

"June, I'd like you to meet Virgil. He's our handyman."

"Handyman." Virgil's face creased even more. It looked like his face might cave in. "Missy, I built this place."

The Master of the Rat's Maze. June wasn't expecting that particular pleasure. "Hi, nice to meet you."

"Virgil is going to build the new phone room, Just as soon as he gets this press working again," Jerry said, again, too loudly.

Virgil decided to argue the point from a better position, so he crawled out from under the press. June thought he would have been better off staying where he was. Virgil was about five foot tall. Jerry Cooper not only had more than a foot on him, but he was also at least twice his weight.

"Look Jerry, I told you this press was a piece of crap. I begged you not to buy it. It will NOT run until you are willing to shell out for this list of expensive replacement parts." He handed Jerry a piece of filthy paper.

Jerry looked dubiously at the list. "No, no, no. We can't get all this stuff at once. How much would you have to spend to get one or two runs out of this machine."

"I already told you." Virgil's scant patience was waning. "I need all this to make it go. Really."

"Alright," Jack suddenly screamed. "You've wasted enough time on this thing for now. Go have some breakfast. Then you can start working on the phone room until I think of something."

For the next hour, June did her best to keep up with Jerry. Trailing after him, she was treated to a tour of the dark room, the screen storage room, and the packing room, which turned out to be the room with all the t-shirts on shelves. Jerry introduced June to all her co-workers along the way.

Everyone seemed cheerfully sarcastic. June wasn't sure if that was good or bad. But none of it was like any other job she had ever had, so June took it as a positive sign.

After the tour, they went back to Jerry's office and tried to write an ad for the new salespeople to go in the newspaper, while dealing with constant interruptions. Jerry insisted on making every decision himself, no matter how trivial.

He just likes being the center of his own little solar system. He thrives on everyone clamoring for his attention, June thought, It was an odd dynamic for such a laid-back place. People found themselves sitting around a good deal, waiting for Jerry to be free to pass judgement. Once Jerry had made all the decisions, there would be a flurry of activity until it was time to make another decision. Then it all came to a standstill again. Jerry had an unusual management style. *Part emperor, part village idiot.*

June was happy when they managed to finish the ad by 3:30, despite Jerry's reluctance to give out any information or spend any money.

"Will we be seeing you again tomorrow," Jerry asked with one eyebrow raised.

June had just been wondering that same thing, but she didn't think she should say so. "Oh yes, I'll be here," she said with a lot more confidence than she felt.

"Good," Jerry replied, unconvinced. "I think you'll like it here if you give it a chance."

June drove home in a fog of indecision.

By the time she got home, she had gone over and over the job in her head. She kept weighing her options, but she just didn't have any. Sure, she could look for another job. She would probably continue to do that anyway. But why not collect a paycheck while looking? She had plenty of time for interviews, if she was offered any, because the hours were so light at Rock Shirt.

As June turned the wheel to enter her street, she was still lost in thought. SLAM. She hit an enormous pothole in the center of the road. The same pothole she had hit dozens of times before.

"Shit. Goddamn. Fucking Shove-It!" June

pounded on the steering wheel and the dash. Abuse like that was the last thing the Chevette needed. And it wasn't the car's fault she hit the pothole. She was turning into a testy bitch, and she didn't like it.

Miracle of miracles, she found a parking space on her block almost directly across from her building. As she parked, she reached to turn down the radio. June had a habit of turning it up loud on her way home from work. It helped to drown out all the noises the Chevette was always making. Especially the squeaking brakes.

All that noise made her nervous. But something was wrong. Where was the volume knob on the radio? June searched the floor but couldn't locate the knob. That was going to be a problem first thing in the morning. It had most likely fallen off when she hit the pothole.

Or when she pounded on the dashboard and cursed a blue streak.

June spent the entire evening lost in a fog, going over it and over it again. As she showered, and put on a set of fuzzy pajamas, reheated some leftover takeout for dinner, and stared at a movie on TV without really watching it, she tried to decide what to do. She finally got the want ads out of the recycling bin and looked at them again.

She had circled three other jobs she hadn't contacted. One was for an accounts receivables clerk at a paper products company. Another was for a receptionist at a large insurance company downtown. The last was for a payroll clerk at an asbestos removal firm. The thought that she might get any of those jobs made her unbearably depressed.

What was the potential for a future with Jack Snow? Jerry had big plans, but what were his odds of success? Even if they filled that room with phones and salespeople, could those two old machines print enough shirts to keep up with that kind of volume? The sensible side of her told her to forget about it.

In spite of everything, June wanted to give Rock Shirt a chance. She wanted to give herself a shot at a job that was, well, fun. It was irresponsible, but maybe that's why she wanted to do it. Shake things up!

As she was getting ready for bed, she had mostly decided to show up tomorrow. She could hang on there for a little while, at least until she could find something that didn't involve asbestos abatement. As soon as she lay down the phone rang.

"Hello?"

"June, it's your mother. What's going on? I tried to call you at work, but the phone was disconnected."

"I was sort of downsized. At least, I feel a lot smaller."

"Oh no, not again. What are you going to do?"

"I already started a new job. Today. It doesn't pay well to start, but it's got a lot of potential," June lied.

"You should probably keep looking."

"Oh I will, but I may as well keep this one for now. Seems like it might be a fun place to work."

Her mother groaned. "That's why it doesn't pay anything. No one will ever pay you to have fun! The reason you get paid for work is that no one in their right mind would ever do it for free."

"You're saying I have nothing but pointless drudgery to look forward to for the next 30 years?"

"That's life… "

"Life's a bitch and then you die." June started laughing.

"I don't see what's so funny."

"It's an inside joke."

"It's hardly a laughing matter. What's wrong with you lately? Are you in love, or something?"

"No! And stop asking me that. I've got to get to bed. Good night, mother."

"Call me."

"Okay. Good bye."

CHAPTER 3

WEDNESDAY, JANUARY 27, 1988

By morning, June had changed her mind again. She dressed in her interview suit and made herself a mug of strong black coffee. She decided a day of job hunting would help her decide one way or the other. Rock Shirt was a shaky ledge to stand on, and as much as she hated to admit it, maybe her mother was right.

She grabbed her coffee and purse and headed out to her car. She thought she would first pick up a paper and check out the want ads. They printed them on Wednesdays, but there were a lot fewer of them than in the Sunday paper. But maybe, if she was very lucky, there would be something new.

She climbed into the Shove-It, and sat staring straight ahead for a minute, trying to clear her head of the thousand thoughts running around up there in combat boots. She took a giant gulp of coffee and turned the ignition key.

The radio started blaring heavy metal music at top volume, causing June to startle jump, sloshing coffee all over her only decent suit. "Shit!" June shrieked. She jumped out of the car as the coffee soaked through and burned her thighs. She waddle-ran back to her apartment to change. Fate had decided for her, she rationalized.

Debbie handed her a notebook as soon as she walked into Jerry's outer office. "People have started calling about the phone jobs," Debbie told her. "You'll have to set appointments until Jerry gets here. You can use his office. I'll transfer the calls to you in there."

June looked at her sideways but didn't protest. A little voice in her head was asking, *Who the hell does she think she is? What exactly IS the chain of command around here?* Jerry seemed to micromanage everything, but when he wasn't around, who had authority?

June opened the heavy door and sat in the big office chair behind Jerry's enormous desk. After a minute of thought, she got up and covered the iguana with one of the many t-shirts scattered all over the office. The phone began ringing persistently, and by the time Jerry finally arrived at 11:00, June had scheduled a full afternoon of interviews.

"Good morning," he chimed happily as he came into the office.

"Hello," smiled June. "We've got interviews beginning at 1:00."

"That's good because we have a lunch meeting with my lawyer at 11:30. I want to check a few things with him about the expansion plans." Jerry suddenly stopped. "Hey! What did you do to my iguana?" He removed the t-shirt and tried to stand the thing up straight.

June shuddered. "It gives me the creeps."

"Leave him alone." He scolded and patted the horrid thing affectionately. "Let's go. I'll drive." June breathed a sigh of relief. She was trying to hide the Shove-It from work people.

As they rode down in the elevator, June noticed Jerry's suit. She kept on noticing it on the walk to the car. Even considering the ugly suits she had seen Jerry wearing over the last few days, this one was the world champ. The material had a patchwork quilt printed on it. It was a loud combination of greens and oranges that made him look like a fat scarecrow.

Jerry's lawyer was waiting for them at a table when they arrived at Bartolatta's Italian Restaurant. He stood up to shake June's hand and Jerry introduced him as Monty. He looked exactly not like a lawyer.

During lunch, Jerry explained his plans to greatly increase sales and production, and Monty stuffed himself with manicotti. June concentrated on following the conversation.

It was just Jerry's version of the work that had been going on at Rock Shirt, but Jerry was answering a lot of June's unanswered questions. It dawned on June that was the reason Jerry brought her to the meeting. He realized she was still on the fence about keeping the job.

Only after completely cleaning his plate, Monty wiped his mouth and began using it for lawyering instead of eating. "Jerry, I still think there are some states you should stay out of, but we've discussed that plenty of times before. My only concern about expanding the business, is that you will get so big that you will become a great enough irritation to the management companies that they come after you to try to stop you."

"They have to catch me first," Jerry grinned.

"True. But right now you are not worth the effort it would take them to find you. If you start to make a LOT of money, they will go to a LOT more trouble to catch you."

"What happens if somebody does catch him," June piped up for the first time.

"They would file a civil lawsuit against him. They'll confiscate the goods in question and any records pertaining to the sale of the goods in question."

"In other words," Jerry interrupted, "we could keep operating. We just wouldn't be able to sell that particular design or designs anymore. Then we drag our feet through the courts for a few years. There is always something new to print. Most things stop being popular so quickly that it isn't worth trying to sue me."

"What about your loyal employees?" June asked the shifty scarecrow.

"None of you will get into any trouble. This is strictly my liability. But the new employees we hire will have to be screened by me personally. Since it's my neck in the noose, so to speak."

"Like you did with me."

Jerry looked at her suspiciously for the first time.

June laughed. "Don't worry. I'm not out to get you. But what if I was? You never even checked my references." Not that June was in a big hurry to have that happen. Why did she say such stupid things?

"I know you're okay. I happen to be a very good judge of people."

June had serious doubts about the logic of that particular conclusion, but she decided against further arguing against the quality of her character.

They had to cut the meeting off quickly because of the interviews June had set up for the afternoon. As it was, they were 10 minutes late, but they could have taken all the time they wanted. The afternoon was plagued by no-shows.

Jerry told her a lot of people changed their minds when they saw the building. June didn't doubt that. She had nearly changed her mind when she saw it for the first time, considering the dogfood smell from up the river and all. They managed to interview several people, however.

The first guy was unemployable. His name was Dean. He was a man in his 50s with a big red nose. He smelled of whiskey and peppermints.

"Dean, do you have a drinking problem?" Jerry came right out and asked him

Dean spilled his guts. He was an alcoholic looking for a break. June squirmed self-consciously and wished she had gone for the job at the asbestos abatement company.

Then Jerry did an astonishing thing. He stood up and shook Dean's hand. "Can you start a week from Monday?"

Jerry HIRED HIM. June wanted to beat Jerry over the head with his iguana, which Dean was trying and failing to ignore. *He probably thinks he's the only one that can see it,* June thought rudely.

Once Dean left the office, June looked at Jerry with astonishment. "I can NOT believe you just hired that guy."

"He'll be good," Jerry insisted. "He just needs a break. He'll be very loyal to us and he won't cause us any trouble. I know. I'm a good judge of character."

"He's a lush."

"We'll give him a chance."

"Jerry, if you want me to help with the interviews, you

need to let me give you my input before you up and hire someone."

"I always hire people that way. I know right away whether someone is going to fit in or not."

"So you don't actually need, or want, my opinion."

Jerry grinned broadly and patted June's head, which June was sure was going to make it explode. "I tell you what. I'll take care of the rest of the interviews. You can go see how Virgil is progressing in the new phone room."

She was so glad to get away from him at that point she didn't complain. But she knew he was just trying to get rid of her. *He's going to hire every freak and weirdy that shows up for an interview, and then he's going to buy me a lion tamer's hat.*

June wound her way through the maze to the new phone room. She found Virgil hauling some old lumber into the empty space. "Hey, Virgil. How's it going?"

"Fair." Virgil grinned at her with bad teeth. "Why are you working for a bastard like Jerry Cooper? You seem like you got more sense than THAT. Hee hee."

June shrugged. "So do you."

"That's where you're wrong, sister," he grinned. "I wouldn't be here but for circumstances. None of us would."

"Circumstances? What do you mean?"

"Take Patti in the packing room. She had a real classy boyfriend several years back, but now he's doing 10 to 15 for racketeering and tax fraud. Patti never worked a day in her life. Now she's in her 50s and having to support herself somehow."

"Are you saying Patti is a gun moll?"

Virgil laughed. "Not exactly. But everybody here suffers from circumstances. We all gotta eat." His face scrunched into a thousand wrinkles when he grinned at her. "So, what's your story then?"

"Sorry to disappoint you, but I don't have any circumstances. Just trying to find a half decent job. We all gotta eat, like you said."

"Then you probably won't be here for very long. Only the truly desperate wind up stuck here."

"How long have you worked for Jerry?" June worried she was asking too many questions, but she was curious. She could never help herself when she was curious. But he just shook his head and laughed.

"I've been here since Jerry started this whole scheme about 4 or 5 years ago, but I've known him longer than that. I've worked for him off and on for the last few centuries."

He didn't give away any secrets about his circumstances, and June felt like he was only telling her the bare minimum. She wanted to ask him what made him so desperate, but she didn't think it would be prudent to ask at this point. She pushed him enough for one day.

Instead, she gave the big, empty room a doubtful look. "Jerry just hired someone and told them to start a week from Monday. Do you think this room will be ready by then?"

"I have NO idea. I shouldn't really start building the cubicles until after the phone company comes in to install all the phone lines. I need to know how many to put where. Do you know if he's talked to the phone company yet?"

"I don't know, but something tells me he hasn't. I better go and remind him."

"Good luck," Virgil chuckled.

Jerry was just coming out of his office with a teenaged girl with blonde hair. He was leering at her in a disturbing way and telling her to come in a week from Monday.

"Hey, Jerry. I talked to Virgil. When are the new phone lines going to be installed?"

"I haven't set that up yet. You can do that now. Tell them we need 20 phone lines installed before next Monday."

Another teenaged girl was waiting to be interviewed. "NEXT," he sang out cheerfully.

Debbie gave June the Mona Lisa smile.

CHAPTER 4

FRIDAY, FEBRUARY 5, 1988

All that week, Jerry interviewed dozens of applicants. They were an assorted bunch of oddballs, which was ironic since the #1 selling shirt that week was for the band, Assorted Oddballs. Terri, the artist, had told June that Jerry had sent someone to the record store to buy it on the day it was released as soon as the store opened. They rushed it back to her so that she could create the art for the silk screens.

She did an amazingly good job. The shirts looked as good as any authentically licensed shirts she had ever seen. Maybe even better.

June made arrangements with the phone company, and they sent a couple of workers to get all the lines installed and operating properly. Then Jerry had June go to the Salvation Army Thrift Store in the Rust Bucket, otherwise known as the Rock Shirt van. It was slightly white, mostly rusty, and full of garbage.

Jerry told her to buy all the old tables, desks, and chairs they had, and to try to get a volume discount. June bit her lip so she didn't laugh at him.

With Virgil's help, it took her four trips to haul everything back to the phone room. The furniture looked even worse in the phone room than it had in the basement of the Salvation Army, but at least everything was serviceable.

June also contacted a company that sold lists of business contacts and phone numbers. She ordered a list that contained nearly every record store in the country. They agreed to rush an order C.O.D. that would get it to her the list first thing Monday morning.

By Friday, the phone room was finished. At least, that's what Virgil claimed. June had never seen anything quite like it. The large brick room had an assorted collection of old desks and tables all around the four walls of the room. Partitions had been built between the desks out of plywood, old doors, bits of wood, and anything else that Virgil could lay his hands on.

June took copies of the most popular shirts and hung them on the partitions and the walls around the room. Every desk had a phone and a metal box full of index cards on it. In the middle of the room was the largest desk – June's desk.

Jerry was hugely pleased. He dragged all the employees from other parts of the maze in to see the finished project. At the end of the day June was tired but happy as she collected her paycheck from Debbie.

She waited until she was sitting in her car before she opened the envelope. It was even worse than she had expected. She was making less than half her salary at her last job.

June sighed heavily and rubbed her tired eyes. She was in too deep now; she knew that. No matter what, she would have to stick it out for a few more weeks. Once the new people got up to speed, and the sales started rolling in, she would start making some decent money. She believed that. She needed to be patient.

The weekend that followed was one of the worst June could ever remember. It started Friday night when June got home from work. She picked up the phone to call her closest friend, Kate, and found that her phone had been disconnected. At least she had been able to pay her electricity bill.

On Saturday morning Kate stopped by. She had her giant coupon wallet and was offering to take June grocery shopping. She had known Kate since grade school, and they were closer than sisters.

Kate was pretty in an unconventional way, and she had a powerful effect on men. Her curly auburn hair and hazel eyes got her noticed, but it was something else that caused men to become obsessed with Kate. June was immune to whatever it was, so June supposed it was what they called 'sex appeal.' June was completely devoid of that trait, she decided.

Kate was popular and had tons of friends. Apart from Kate, June had few friends, none of whom she saw often. At her old apartment she was friends with a few of her neighbors. They used to get together regularly to play cards and drink beer in each other's apartments. When June had moved (well, gotten evicted for not paying the rent) they all said they would keep in touch, but it never happened.

Kate scolded June as soon as she opened the door. "What's going on? Your phone is disconnected again. I have been trying to call you at work, but I found out you no longer have a job at Schlink & Busboom. They told me you were 'no longer in their employ.' How did you get fired this time?"

"I'd really rather not talak about it," June tried to change the subject. "That supervisor had it in for me from the beginning. Thanks for taking me shopping. I just got paid, but I need to spend as little as possible. Just enough to keep from starving."

As they shopped, June told Kate all about Rock Shirt. Kate listened carefully, nodded a lot, but didn't offer any opinions until they were back in Kate's car and headed home. "June, this is the craziest story you have ever come up with. You can NOT be serious about working at that place."

"I AM serious about it," June suddenly erupted. "I need to give this a try. I know it sounds sketchy, but the lawyer guy says I'm not liable for anything, even if we get caught. Jerry says we won't. We aren't worth the effort."

"I think it's a big mistake. Why don't you move into my place for a couple of months? Just so you can save for a security deposit and look for a decent job," Kate offered. "This kind of thing isn't like you."

"Let's not argue about it. Thank you for the offer. I sincerely appreciate it, really. But I need to give this a few weeks. I need to try it. If I bomb out, I am not out anything but a little time. I will be careful. You know how level-headed I am."

"I do, and that's why I don't understand this at all." Kate shook her head and sighed. "Let me know if you need to get out of there quick." She laughed, "Or if you need a bus ticket out of town."

"Thanks, but don't worry. Everything's going to be fine." June wished she felt as confident as she sounded.

Kate suggested they go out for dinner and drinks, but June turned her down. She was far too broke. Anyway, she wasn't feeling festive.

June spent the weekend trying to figure out how to get her paycheck to last an entire week. She could make rent, but she was going to be hungry.

Maybe she could get Jerry to take her for a business lunch. If she brought home a doggy bag, she might be able to manage it. She could be convincing when she was hungry. He owed her. He never said anything about starvation wages.

On Sunday night she opted for graham crackers and tea for dinner. She had a restless night. She dreamt she was being chased by a giant iguana, just like in Journey to the Center of the Earth.

CHAPTER 5

MONDAY, FEBRARY 8, 1988

June set the coffee mug she brought from home on the enormous surface of her new desk. There was also a wire basket labeled "ORDERS," and a small ivy plant she had moved from the outer office.

She couldn't help but grin broadly as she sat in her large, once leather office chair and spun completely around once. It was once leather, but now it was mostly duct tape, but it still seemed kind of fancy by Rock Shirt standards.

It's a bit like having a desk in the middle of a soccer field, June thought, *but it will be different once the room is full of people.*

Jerry had hired 11 people so far, and he was still actively interviewing candidates. Plus the 3 orphans from the old phone closet made 14. She had gotten to know them a bit since she had first met them on the day of her interview.

Derek was Jerry's 'star' salesman. At least, that was how he referred to himself. June hated him immediately. It was obvious that he wasn't overly fond of June either. He resented her authority and was publicly dismissive of her attempts to train them on phone sales. So far they had managed to keep the peace by avoiding each other.

The second telemarketer was a chatty young woman named Beth. She told June all about Cathy, the third member of the phone crew. According to Beth, Cathy was 19 and had three kids. Cathy worked for Jerry under the table so she could continue to collect her welfare benefits.

"Really?" June expressed surprise at that bit of gossip.

"You don't expect her to live just off welfare, do you?" Beth suddenly defended Cathy. "They hardly give you anything!"

June wondered why Jerry didn't pay Cathy enough so she could get off welfare all together, but she didn't think she should say so out loud. June didn't know what it was like to be a single mother, but she imagined it to be a difficult existence. She could discuss it with Jerry, but she didn't believe he would tell her the truth. She wasn't sure she wanted to know all the details anyway.

After meeting the three of them, June decided they should be included in the training session she had planned for the new employees' first day. She was expecting delivery of the sales list she had ordered, and that would give her newly trained group an opportunity to make their first cold calls before the end of the day.

Everything had been planned to her satisfaction, and she sat at her desk extra early. Too early. She absent-mindedly checked her new little ivy and decided it needed a drink of water.

She took the little potted plant into the bank of restrooms behind Rock Shirt. While she started to water the ivy at the tap, she noticed a large watering can under the sink. June filled the can until overflowing, and then struggled to carry it, and her ivy back to the office. She was just starting to water all the plants in the outer office when Jerry came through the door.

"You're watering the plants? I love that," Jerry enthused and then unlocked the carved wooden door to his office and swung it open. "Would you water the ones in my office too, please?"

June followed him into his office. "They are half-dead. I hope they all come back."

"You can take care of all the plants for me. They need help," he moaned. "They all look terrible."

"Who takes care of them now?"

"Nobody."

"That explains a lot."

"PLEASE would you do it for me?" Jack whined plaintively.

"Oh all right," June hurriedly agreed. "Just please stop doing that."

Jerry chuckled and looked pleased with himself. June rolled her eyes.

They both heard something and looked at each other. "Someone is calling for help out in the hall." Jerry ran to the front office and propped open the outer door. "New people in here," he yelled down the corridor in a booming voice.

June sighed and put down the watering can. The plants would have to wait, the poor dears. She went to find where the newbies had wandered off.

She found Dean in one of the dead ends behind the print room and led him back to the phone room. She told him to pick out a desk and take a seat, and then headed to the elevator.

She decided to wait for people on the ground floor so she didn't lose anybody. She directed those arriving up to the third-floor phone room until 9:35, five minutes after they were all supposed to arrive, and then headed back upstairs. People were chatting in small groups and choosing their desks. Everyone was talking at once.

"Your attention please," June shouted over the din. "Good morning, everyone. My name is June, and I am the Sales Manager here at Rock Shirt." They all knew that already, but she wanted them all to recognize her as the authority in the room. She hoped she had the gravitas to pull off her new 'boss' role. "Let's get started by having you all introduce yourselves."

Just then, Derek came in from the corridor and removed his Ray-Bans. "Hey, where do I sit?"

"Anywhere," June began. "We've started…"

"I want a desk by the window."

"Just pick an empty chair."

"I should get first pick. This is bullshit."

June felt her authority slipping. Gravitas? Forget about it. "We'll discuss it later. Just sit down." June sounded as exasperated as she felt.

"I don't need to sit through any training. I know what I'm doing. Just let me get going on my calls so I can make some commission."

"Everybody can benefit from a little training. It's no reflection on you. We should all be working on the same goals. So please, just sit down and shut up."

June regretted the 'shut up' as soon as it left her mouth,

but Derek was trying to disrupt her and make her look foolish. She was not going to have that.

"Who do you think you are, you pushy bitch? You're not my boss."

June took a deep breath and tried to speak calmly. "Yes. I. Am. I am the new sales manager."

"I don't have to take orders from you. I'm going to talk to Jerry." Derek left in a huff.

June took a deep breath and plowed ahead. "Let's start those introductions, shall we?" She did her best to smile at the group. "Where should we start?"

June looked around the room and wondered what in hell Jerry had been thinking when he hired them. The majority of the group were cute teenaged girls, but it also included a very small, very wrinkled old woman, and Dean, who was looking radiantly sober.

June pointed at a desk in one of the corners of the room. "Let's start here!" June pointed at a cute Asian woman who told the group her name was Ann.

Next to Ann was Cliff, a slick looking white guy wearing expensive clothes and carrying a calfskin briefcase. He spent a lot of time chatting up Ann. On the other side of him was Julie, a high school aged girl who, it turned out, was the artist, Terri's daughter.

Another of the young women was Sharon, a bleach-blonde with teeth like a horse, and a vacant expression that suggested she had an IQ to match. June rudely thought she looked like Mortimer Snerd.

Seated near the door was a young black man with glasses and a head full of little dreadlocks. His name was Leo.

June made sure they all had several copies of the list of shirts Debbie had given June on her first day. It seemed like ages had passed since that day.

June cleared her throat and began. "Rock Shirt is a bootleg t-shirt company," she started. "We sell all the hottest shirts cheaper than anybody else because all of our original designs are unlicensed. If people ask you why our shirts are so cheap, you tell them that they are bootleg. If they ask you outright if they are bootleg, you say YES."

Murmurs around the room began to get louder. "The reason we do this is so that we are not guilty of defrauding the public. We are being honest. So we can't get in trouble with the law! Our fearless leader, Jerry, can be sued for damages, but we are not personally responsible for any of that."

June looked around the group and noticed one of the new people, a middle-aged lady named Kelly, slip out the door.

"Looks like we lost one," June smiled at the group. A few chuckles, but more than a few nervous groans. "Is there anyone else concerned about the legality of working for this kind of business?"

A couple people raised their hands, and then a couple more. Then a lot more. "I think it would be better if you heard it directly from the boss. I'll get Jerry and he can explain the ramifications to you all."

June hurried to Jerry's office. She couldn't convince them it was all perfectly safe for them to work there when she wasn't entirely sure of it herself. As she approached the outer office, June could hear Derek arguing with Debbie.

"Nobody can see Jerry right now," Debbie was saying. "It will just have to wait." She had her hands on her hips and she was standing down Derek. She looked tiny compared to him, but he was not about to cross her.

"If I don't talk to him right now then I'm walking!" he threatened. Then he noticed June. "Tell Jerry I quit!" he yelled loud enough that Jerry couldn't fail to hear him. Then he stomped out the door and slammed it hard enough to rattle the glass.

Debbie cringed, and then turned to June with irritation. "Jerry is going to be so pissed at you."

"What did I do?"

"You made his star salesman quit."

June snorted. "Frankly, I think we're better off. What's up with Jerry? Is the lawyer here or what?"

Debbie just rolled her eyes. "Trust me. You don't want to know."

"Is Jerry even in there?"

"Yeah, but don't go in! You can't talk to him right now."

June was starting to see red. "Look…" she began.

Just then the heavy wooden door swung open, and a teenage girl came out, followed by Jerry. The girl looked nervous, and something else. Afraid? Embarrassed?

"Debbie," Jerry called. He then noticed June standing there and looked startled. "What do you want?" he asked June.

"I need you to reassure the new people. I'm afraid half of them may walk out before we even get started on the training."

"I'll be right there," he waved his hand at her dismissively and turned back to Debbie. "Make out a payroll check for this lady for 25, no wait, make that $27.83."

The girl giggled. "A tip!"

Debbie pulled out the checkbook ledger as June watched Jerry's back retreat down the hall. She realized that the uneven dollar amount made it a lot less obvious that Jerry was paying his hookers with payroll checks.

June hurried down the hall after Jerry, but she quickly lost sight of him. She decided to get back to the phone room and wait for him there.

When she walked through the door from the hallway, she was amazed at how loud it was in the big room. Everyone was wandering around and chatting amiably in small groups. She was happy to see that everyone was getting along, and she thought the room looked much better without Derek in it.

A couple of the younger women came in from the hall with cans of soda and bags of snacks. She noticed several people had hit a vending machine or something during the unscheduled break. June quickly asked them both, "Where are the vending machines?"

"Beth showed us how to get to Honor Snacks, on the ground floor," the shorter girl said. Her name was Crystal

"They have all the stuff in crates, and you pick out what you want and it's only a quarter!" the taller girl enthused. Her name was Diane.

June was thinking that 25 cents for snacks sounded like an amazing deal. A few quarters for lunch were about all she could afford right now. Honor Snacks was a company that sold snacks in offices all over the city, but they didn't use vending machines. As the name implied, they had a cash box with the snacks and people were supposed to pay on the 'honor system.'

"JUNE," Jerry suddenly boomed from the front office.

June hurried down the inner hallway that snaked between offices until she was back in the Debbie zone.

Jerry was red in the face. The color clashed badly with his olive-green suit. He saw her and waved his ballpoint pen like a sword in her direction. "What is this? C.O.D. for $325! Are you CRAZY?"

June had never seen Jerry get really angry. He had never yelled at her before. It was like being mauled by Winnie the Pooh.

"I told you about it last week," June managed to stammer.

"WHEN?"

"You remember, I said that all these new people were going to need something to do when they started."

"You can get phone books for free from the phone company." Jerry was still bellowing.

"We discussed this. That isn't at ALL practical. They don't have phone books from around the country waiting to hand them out. We talked about ordering a list of record stores. All the record stores in the country. The list will more than pay for itself by the end of the DAY."

June tried to sound completely sure of herself. She would not cry. She would not fall to pieces. Hopefully. "Otherwise, you will be paying all those people in there to sit around pretending to make sales calls."

Jerry looked like he was calming down. He bounced the package in his hands, testing its weight. "All of them?" he looked at June sideways.

"Everyone."

Jerry handed the package to June and then, over his shoulder to Debbie he said quietly, "Pay him."

Jerry put his arm around June's back and led her down the hall and back to the phone room. "What's this about people walking out?"

"They heard the word 'bootleg' and it made them nervous. I explained that they were in no personal jeopardy, but I think they want to hear it from you."

When they entered the noisy room, June hurried to regain everyone's attention. June had a skill she didn't often display on the job. She had a fierce ballfield whistle. She didn't even use her fingers. She curled her tongue sharply and gave a loud blast.

Everyone shut up. Jerry spun around and looked at June, amazed.

She cleared her throat and tried not to blush. "Everyone, take your seats. Jerry has some things to clarify for all of you."

June thought it best to just soldier on. She smiled and gestured to Jerry to take over. He was still looking at her with a goofy expression she couldn't interpret, but he smiled at the group and began.

"Good morning, good morning!" he began cheerfully. "You probably already know that my name is Jerry, and I am the owner of Rock Shirt, the best bootleg shirt company in America! We have the best shirts at the best prices, and the nicest salespeople in the business!"

Blech, June thought. *He's laying it on too thick. Get on with it already, Jerry.*

"But because we are bootleg, there are a few precautions I would like you to take, to protect me, your lovable boss, and also to protect all our jobs! We can keep this company rolling if we all follow a few rules."

"First," Jerry continued, "do not use my real name over the phone to any of our customers. When making sales calls, you should use my alias – Jack Snow."

Several people laughed.

"I know it sounds funny, but it will help to keep us up and running. It is a necessary precaution. That's all."

"What happens if we get caught?" someone asked.

"Nothing will happen to any of you. You will all be

perfectly safe, but I will be sued, and there may come a point when I need to close or move the company. So, we want to avoid that situation."

"You must never, EVER, give out our street address, he continued. "You will notice there is a PO Box number on the top of our shirt list. This is the address you are to use. Are there any other questions?"

Myrtle raised her hand, so Jerry pointed at her. "When do we get paid?" she had the croakiest voice June had ever heard. Several people tittered.

"We all want to know that," Cliff hollered.

"At the end of the day on Fridays. The sooner you start selling, the sooner we can all start getting rich," Jerry said jovially.

June had her doubts that anybody was going to get rich from t-shirts, but for the moment she was happy to go along with the dream. They gave Jerry a smattering of applause and he quickly retreated down the hallway.

"Okay!" she said to the group. "Let's get this training started. Can I get a volunteer to be a customer? I will show you how to get your customers started."

No volunteers. She should have expected that.

"Beth, you've done this before. You know the things people say to you when you call, so why don't I pretend to call you and sell you some shirts."

Beth got up and came to the middle of the room. June smiled at her. "This will be easy, she told her. Start off being an easy customer. Then we will do a second one, and you give me every excuse you ever heard, alright?"

"Yeah, okay!" Beth liked the idea. It was like she was in on something.

I think I might get the hang of this, if I don't make Jerry mad and get fired first, June thought.

CHAPTER 6

WEDNESDAY, JUNE15, 1988

As is typical for Milwaukee, winter hung on much longer than anyone expected. There was about a week of spring rain before the temperature hit 80 degrees and summer started ahead of schedule. Mosquito-filled humidity sat on the city and refused to allow in a breeze off the lake.

June told her friend Kate that she liked her job, but sometimes she wondered why. Jerry was so condescending, and he constantly undermined her authority.

He had called Derek and convinced him to come back to work by telling him that June would have no authority over him and would leave him completely alone. June was furious, but there was no reasoning with Jerry.

Jerry believed Derek was worth it because he was such

a good salesman. June had yet to witness anything to convince her of that. She decided to make the best of the situation by openly pretending Derek was invisible. This irritated Derek and amused Jerry more than June had hoped.

After a few weeks, it became apparent that Derek was NOT a star salesman. He may have been good when there were only two other salespeople, but in a room full of hungry people, he wasn't even in the top half.

June felt like her training was really paying off, but the little voice in the back of her head that calls her a fraud said the shirts sold themselves. They were wildly popular with high school kids, and they were high profit for the customers thanks to the ridiculously low prices.

Everybody was making decent money now. The phones were filled, and Jerry was still toying with the idea of a second shift. June told him there was no point until he increased production. That second press was still broken more often than not, and Jerry reluctantly agreed.

June really liked most of the people she was working with. Ann, Leo, and Sharon asked June to go out with them for a beer after work after they had known her only a few days.

Despite her better judgement she had started to become close friends with the three of them. The gang in the phone room accepted her as one of their own, rather than as the boss. She was more the head inmate than the warden.

Jerry was not very good at delegating authority. He liked having people chase him around just to get him to make the simplest decision, like what to print next. June could NOT understand why they didn't have a run list with at least a day or two on it. He wouldn't because "what's hot changes too fast." June had her doubts about Jerry's pronouncements, and this one seemed very fishy.

The only real problem June could see with her current situation, was her growing infatuation with Leo. His light Jamaican accent was starting to drive her to distraction, not to mention his big, brown eyes. She knew it was a bad idea to date people you work with, but when you were the person's supervisor it was just plain wrong.

She did her best to act casually around him and hoped it was just a passing infatuation. She was starting to get to know him pretty well, and it seemed to be getting worse instead of better, but she was working on it. Not that it mattered anyway, she told herself. He didn't seem to be interested in her that way.

June had other things to worry about. Her Chevette had been stalling out at inconvenient times for a couple months now. June would have gotten it fixed, but it had so MANY things wrong with it she decided it wasn't worth spending the money on it. Instead of making a decision about it, she just kept driving the Shove-It.

Why was it so hard for her to shift gears in her life? She had always avoided making decisions, instead waiting until the situation changed organically. It was like she was born with terminal procrastination about all the important things in her life.

It was the middle of June, and things were starting to click in the phone room. Most of the gang were making decent money for such short hours. Everyone was happy to be working, there and that made June's job much easier.

By the time she got in, the place was already jumping, and she had a pile of orders filling the Inbox on her desk. Things were going very well, indeed. Cliff had started coming in early and he started a trend among the more competitive phone people.

Sharp dressing Cliff was a car salesman that had been out of work for a while. (Two years according to Beth, the phone room gossip.) He took the job with Jerry out of desperation. He couldn't WAIT to find something else. Anything else. His superior attitude made him pretty unpopular around the phone room, but June couldn't fault his work. He sold a lot of shirts.

"Good morning, June," said Leo as he placed another order in the bin.

June smiled at Leo before saying loudly, "Hello, everyone." She was playing it cool except for the blushing.

Jerry came into the phone room waving a t-shirt in the air. "New shirts to start selling today: Commence Testing, Inferno Girls, Graveyard Shift, and Stark Nekkid. Sell them while they're hot!"

Jerry dropped the new shirts on June's desk. "June, I need to talk to you about your commission."

June felt an ice-cold chill. Then she noticed Debbie standing behind Jerry wearing her Mona Lisa face.

"Okay, let's go to your office," June suggested.

They headed down the hall with Debbie tagging along behind them. June hoped Debbie wouldn't follow them into Jerry's office, but Jerry didn't go into his office. Instead, he sat on Debbie's desk.

"Debbie, get out the payroll book," he said. "Take a seat," he said to June.

"What's going on, Jerry?" June didn't want to sit down.

"I'm going to have to start paying you commission on what gets shipped out instead of what gets sold."

"Oh no, Jerry," June shook her head. "You can't do

that. That wasn't our agreement."

"Your phone people keep selling weird stuff we don't have time to print."

It was funny how they were now 'June's phone people.'

"Is it my fault your expansion plan didn't include enough production to support the sales?"

"We finally got the other machine running. We WILL catch up. Just don't let those people sell junk. Tell them to push the new stuff."

"If we have 'junk' on the shirt list, we should take the junk off the list. We haven't had Rural Americans in stock ever, as far as I can tell. Why is it still on the list?"

"We need to keep everything on the list. Just don't sell it," he insisted illogically while waving dismissively at her.

"Don't you dare cut my commission, Jerry. I will have a talk with all the phone people. They can call some of the worst offenders back and convince them to take the new shirts instead. They will push Stark Nekkid. I promise."

"Okay. We'll look at it at the end of the week," he agreed and made a face at Debbie.

"How interesting," June thought as she went back to the phone room and the growing pile of orders on her desk. She sat down and sorted through them. It seemed like only a few people were taking all the orders for the junk shirts.

The biggest offender was Myrtle. She had just taken an order for Rural Americans. June groaned. She hated talking to Myrtle one-to-one.

Myrtle was about 80 with a shaky voice. For some reason, this made her incredibly popular as a salesperson for the shirts with dirty sayings on them. There was something amusing about hearing a grandmotherly voice telling you to 'Eat Shit, & Die.'

In person, Myrtle was less fun. She was about 4'11'' and she would stand right under June's nose and shout up into her face. Myrtle wasn't hard of hearing, and neither was June, so this seemed odd.

Myrtle's dentures didn't fit properly, so when she talked her teeth clacked like castanets, but not in time with what she was saying. Myrtle also had an acid stomach and chewed antacid tablets all day, she always had a white, chalky ring around the sides of her mouth. While she was talking she would belch the occasional word.

Myrtle would stand under June's nose, shouting and clicking and belching. June would get so caught up with all the sound effects, she couldn't follow the conversation.

Instead of talking to Myrtle, June decided on a general announcement first. Maybe she wouldn't need to talk to Myrtle at all. A girl could dream.

"ATTENTION EVERYONE," June bellowed her loudest.

Her shouting had no effect whatsoever. She climbed onto her desk and unleashed the whistle. "TWEET!"

People stopped talking and turned to stare. Mouths hung open. At least she had their attention.

"I have an announcement to make that effects everyone's commission." Now she REALLY had their attention.

"I know you want to sell as much as you can, but please don't sell things we don't have in stock. Believe me when I say your order for a dozen shirts will not convince Jerry to print Rural Americans. If you are not sure what we have in stock, take a field trip down the hall to the packing room and take a look."

"Some of your orders from this morning will need to

be changed," June continued. "I will be bringing them around. Please call them back and say, 'This thing you ordered is a dud. We got new shirts in today that will sell like crazy' You are doing them a favor. Do you all get it?"

"YES," was said by all with varying levels of enthusiasm. June climbed awkwardly down from her desk, only to look up and see Leo grinning at her.

"Nice view," he commented with that accent. June could not stop herself from blushing all the way to her toes. So much for being cool.

She hurried over to Myrtle's desk even though she wasn't in a hurry to talk to Myrtle. "Hi Myrtle. I need you to call these people back." June put the order on her desk.

"Why? Click."

"Because several things are not in stock. I have marked them for you. Just have them take the new stuff."

"But you don't understand," Myrtle began a Spike Jones symphony. June didn't get any of it.

"I don't know what to tell you." That much was true. "Even if they order them, they won't get them. Then Jerry will come to you and demand his commission back because he is a slimy rat."

Myrtle was no fool. She was at Rock Shirt to make money. She took the form and went back to her phone.

One of Dean's orders also needed correcting. June took it over to him and pointed out the offending designs. She noticed he smelled strongly of peppermint. She looked him in the eyes, but he looked alright. Anyway, it was only 10:30 in the morning, but June made a mental note to keep an eye on Dean.

About mid-afternoon, Dean lurched past her on the way back to his desk, and June was pretty certain he was stewed. *He must have a bottle hidden somewhere*, she thought. He was never gone for long, so he must have it hidden nearby.

June decided she needed to talk to Jerry about it. She honestly wished he would fire Dean, but she wasn't hopeful he would. His sales were not great, but they weren't terrible either, and he had some loyal accounts.

June headed for Jerry's office and found the carved door ajar. June walked in. "Hi Jerry."

Jerry was standing alone behind his desk. On the desk was a metal file box. Looking into the metal box was an iguana. In the metal box was a great deal of cash. June had never seen a box of money before.

Her brain was having trouble comprehending what she was seeing; it froze and refused to respond so she stood there with a very stupid expression.

Jerry suddenly slammed the box closed. June just stood there, blinking.

"I am burying $50,000 in my basement," Jerry laughed nervously.

June realized she did NOT want to know. She changed the subject. "Dean's getting drunk."

"What, now?"

"Yeah. He must have a bottle somewhere."

He thought about it for 30 seconds. "Have him followed," he finally decided.

"By whom, pray tell?"

"Pick someone you can trust. Not that car guy."

"You mean somebody from the phone room?"

"Yeah."

"You are crazy."

"I'm not going to fire him. Just have somebody watch him for a while and he will straighten out. Otherwise, I will have a talk with him"

June went back to the phone room and sat at her desk. She was staring at nothing when she realized Leo was talking to her.

"Everybody is goin' to the Crazy Shepard tonight. Peg's band is playing You want to come wid us?"

"Peg in the print room plays in a band? What's it called?"

"The Popping Cherries."

June laughed. "Okay, thanks." She grinned like an eejit, and she told herself to get a grip. Leo wasn't asking her out on a date. She was just going out with the whole group from work.

"How many can you fit in your car?" Leo asked her as Ann and Sharon finished their work and joined them at the center desk.

June's heart nearly stopped. "Ummmm…not counting me? Two uncomfortably, three painfully, and four with some minor internal injuries." She prayed no one would really take her up on it.

"Good," Ann laughed. "Then you can take those of us with medical insurance."

"None of us has insurance," Sharon puzzled as Ann's joke flew over her head. "We all work here."

June would never live down the ride to the club that night in the Shove-It. She tried to discourage them, but they squeezed three people into the backseat anyway. June would have been happy that Leo was riding up front with her, but her floorboards were so rusty, that when he got in, he put his foot straight through the floor.

Worst of all, the Chevette stalled as June was making a left turn at a traffic light. She restarted it and cleared the intersection, but the screams from her passengers in the tight confines of the car made June's ears ring before the band had even started.

They arrived at the club with a celebratory air, due to their having come through a traumatic experience together. *That was why the employees of Rock Shirt had a special camaraderie*, June realized. *It was the direct result of shared misery.*

The Popping Cherries had a diverse but loyal following of screaming fans. Everyone was there, including Terri the artist, and her daughter Julie, the packing room crew, and both shifts from the printing room. Jerry had given them the night off. Even Jerry showed up and bought a round to thunderous applause.

June was standing near the bar when Julie approached her. "LOOK, Jerry's dancing with Terri!"

"Where?" June scanned the crowd.

"Right there," she pointed. "I can't believe the way he dances." She laughed loudly and then ran to tell another group of employees standing nearby. June wasn't as interested in what Julie had said as she was in the way that she said it.

June moved to where Debbie was standing with her husband, Chip. "Excuse me," June said. "I hope I'm not interrupting anything. Can I ask you a question?"

Debbie smirked. "Yes you are, and yes you can. What is it?"

"I thought that Julie was Terri's daughter."

"She is."

"That's funny because I just heard Julie call Terri by her first name. Is Terri her step-mother?"

"No. Terri is Julie's father. Or should I say 'was' her father. I don't know. They don't have a name for that one yet." Chip snorted and giggled like crazy.

They are both wasted, June thought. "Are you saying

Terri used to be a man?"

"Yes. But now he's a she."

June couldn't believe it. Terri was more feminine than she was.

Circumstances.

Terry had undeniable talent, but she worked for Jerry because of circumstances. Virgil was right. June looked around the group through beer goggles. All of them were kind-hearted and decent people when all was said and done.

Well, maybe not Debbie. But everybody else.

At bar time they all tried to sing Roll Out the Barrel. June took a cab home.

CHAPTER 7

THURSDAY, JUNE 23, 1988

June was pondering 'Operation Dean' as she watered the plants. She had trouble asking other people to do things she was reluctant to do herself. Spying on Dean was hypocritical, immoral, and obnoxious, so she had to do it herself.

She was an utter failure as a spy. She had been so busy the first two days, Dean had gotten very drunk without June ever noticing he had left the room.

On the third day she actually tried to follow him. He took her on a tour of the catacombs, but she lost him somewhere in the basement. He must have known he was being followed, but she had been so careful. As she rode back up to the 3rd floor in the freight cage, she decided she needed to ask for some help.

The plants in the office had started to respond to June's

TLC and plant food. The plant on the corner of Debbie's desk was particularly vigorous in its comeback. It had spread out to cover nearly half the desk.

June moved into Jerry's office to water the plants in there. While she was watering, she looked at all the odds and ends Jerry had collected during his travels around the world. He had a predilection for little boxes. One was hand-carved Javanese camphor wood, and one was Chinese inlay. There was a plastic one that looked like he bought it at 7 Mile Flea Market, but maybe it had sentimental value.

Then June noticed a small picture frame hanging on the wall, half concealed by a hanging plant. It was a photograph of a car. As June moved closer, she realized it was a picture of a DeLorean, and it was parked in the snow. It had a bumper sticker that said, "Things go better with Coke." Of course.

I get it, she thought. *I'm not THAT dumb*. Jerry's alias made a lot more sense, and some of his odd behavior.

She was still staring at the picture when Jerry arrived.

"You're spilling," he yelled, startling her. At least she stopped absent-mindedly pouring water on the carpet. "Use these," he said and handed her one of the many piles of t-shirts that seemed to be everywhere.

June dropped them on the puddle and began wiping up the mess.

"I am glad to see you watering. OH MY GOD," he shrieked. "This one has bloomed."

Peg had just come into the office and laughed at Jerry's enthusiasm. She was wearing a shirt that said Thousands Die Screaming. "What next, Jerry?"

"Inferno," he told her, and she ran off to print Inferno.

Out of the corner of her eye, June saw something

moving across Jerry's desk. Her first thought was that she had gotten water on the iguana, and it had rehydrated. Miraculously revived, it was trying to escape and was headed for the door.

June screamed.

The crawling object, which June realized was too hairy to be an iguana, headed straight for Jerry and leapt up at him.

June screamed again.

"Would you quit scaring my dog. What's wrong with you?" Jerry bellowed.

"DOG?"

"His name is Mosquito. He's a long-haired Chihuahua." The dog was licking all over Jerry's face and shaking spasmodically.

"Ewwwwww."

"I had to pick him up at the vet. Don't you like dogs?"

"Dogs? Yes. Not sure about that thing, though."

"He hasn't had anything to eat yet. Run down to La Bourgeoisie and ask the chef for some scraps."

"What do you mean, scraps," June asked suspiciously.

"Just tell them what you want them for, and he'll give you some leftovers."

"I am not going begging for scraps for your dog!" June was horrified.

"They know me there. It will be alright. I do it all the time."

"Then you can do it again," June insisted.

"You do it," he bellowed. Jerry was getting exasperated, but not half as exasperated as June.

"No way!"

"I have too much to do," Jerry insisted. "The lawyer is coming today. PLEASE."

"Does he have to eat gourmet? Can't I just get him a happy meal or something?"

"No. Now go." He physically shoved June out of the office and shut the door.

June walked back to the phone room just as Dean was arriving for the day. "Dean," she called to him as sweetly as she could. "I need you to go over to that French place and ask for some scraps for Jerry's dog."

"Are you kidding?"

"I only wish I was. This is a very important job. Jerry's dog is very delicate. Pure breed, you know."

June wanted to get rid of Dean for a little while, and why not kill two birds. He eyed her suspiciously but left right away.

June then called a meeting at her desk. She included the people she considered to be her friends: Leo, Ann, Sharon, and Charlie. This wasn't the kind of thing she liked to ask of her friends, but she felt like her options were limited.

Charlie was a long-haired, freaky guy with a wicked sense of humor. He was new, but he had joined up with their little group almost immediately.

June sighed before she started. "Dean has been getting drunk every day. Does anybody know where he hides his bottle?"

Ann laughed. "Could be anywhere. There are a million places to hide in this building."

"I need to have him watched. Discretely."

"We can do it!" Charlie seemed to get a kick out of the idea.

"I hate to even ask, but Jerry won't do anything unless we can find a bottle. And even then he won't fire him."

"We'll get it," Charlie said with confidence that June

did not share.

"Don't let him see you, or we'll have to call the whole thing off."

"It will be a snap," Ann laughed. "We've all gotten pretty good at navigating the corridors."

They all snickered, and June felt like she was missing the joke. "What's going on? You all look like you're up to something."

"June's never seen it," Sharon blurted. Everyone tried to shush her, but it was a bit late for that.

"What haven't I seen?"

They all looked at each other and then looked at their shoes.

"Leo," June met his eyes, and it took him a moment to decide what to do.

"Come on, den. I'll show you." Leo took June's hand, and then addressed the rest of the group. "Meet us dare when you can. Don't you all leave at once!"

June went with Leo and all kinds of conflicting emotions. "Where are we going?"

But Leo just put his finger to his lips. He was cryptically quiet as he led June to a section of the third floor that was unused. In the back of an empty office was a door that led to a staircase. June waited to see if they were going up or down, but Leo did neither.

"What are you trying to show me?" June wished Leo was still holding her hand.

Leo just looked at her and grinned. "It's our own little breakroom, but you can tell no one. It's a secret."

"Breakroom?" June puzzled over the disused staircase and Leo laughed.

He walked over to the back wall and pushed against it. The whole wall moved back an inch and became a sliding panel. He pushed it aside to reveal a hidden room in the back corner of the old warehouse. It had windows on two sides that overlooked the river and a drawbridge crossing it.

June rushed in, astonished, as Leo joined her and pushed the wall back into place. They had dragged in some abandoned furniture, a table and several shabby chairs. The room was littered with empty soda cans and cigarette butts. "How long have you all been using this place?"

"A few weeks." June realized Leo was holding his breath, waiting for June's reaction.

She laughed. He still looked unsure.

There was a tap on the wall, and the rest of the group joined them. *All at once*, June noticed. Everyone grabbed a seat, obviously comfortable with the surroundings. Ann handed June a can of soda.

"Thanks." June popped the top and looked out at the river. The room had an amazing view. What an odd little spot. *If there are places like this in the building,* she thought, *no wonder we haven't been able to find Dean.*

While she was lost in thought, Sharon pulled a joint out of her bra and lit it. They all gasped audibly as Sharon handed it to June.

June looked at the four of them and took a hit. She was answered by a loud sigh of relief from all of them. They were taking a big chance by trusting her, June realized, but she was taking a bigger chance by trusting them.

"Does Dean know about this room?" June asked doubtfully.

"No, of course not," said Ann as she passed the joint to Leo. "We're the only ones that know about it."

The four of them were June's closest friends at Rock Shirt. It seemed weird to know that they had been keeping this secret from her because of her position as sales manager.

"You know, I have to fire all of you now."

They all held their breath while June tried to keep a straight face.

"Just kidding!" she finally said.

"Sharon erupted with a loud donkey laugh. "And Jerry said June was straight enough to shit yardsticks."

CHAPTER 8

FRIDAY, JUNE 24, 1988

June was very late getting to work. Charlie was looking for her and caught up with her in the hall as she arrived.

"We are all ready to follow Dean today. Don't worry. This time we'll catch him." He grinned broadly and tugged on his ponytail.

June groaned. "I've changed my mind about that. I want you to forget the whole thing." June was having pangs of guilt. "Tell the others I'm calling it off."

"Why?" Charlie sounded disappointed.

"Don't you think it's a tad hypocritical? I mean," she shifted from one foot to the other. "Don't you feel guilty about spying on him?"

"No," Dean was surprised. "We're trying to help him. Jerry's not going to fire him."

"That's true," June admitted. "But I would still feel like a creep."

At midday, June and Leo were sitting on her desk and talking when Jerry came into the phone room with a batch of new shirts.

"ATTENTION," he bellowed. "Starting today you can now sell Inflatable Girls. And we have two new sayings on shirts. 'I Love Animals – They're Delicious,' and 'I Don't Know Whether to Commit Suicide or Go Bowling.' That one is very popular locally."

Debbie was following in Jerry shadow again. As usual, she looked like she had a nasty secret.

"Dat girl is trouble," Leo commented in June's ear.

"I need to make an important announcement," Jerry continued. "Listen up," he boomed. "This being Friday, I know you are all expecting your paychecks after work, as usual."

"Uh oh," June felt a rush of panic.

"Be careful what you say next, Jerry," someone heckled.

"Checks WILL be ready today, but due to a cash flow problem, checks will now be distributed at 6:00 pm instead of at 3:30 when you finish your shift."

"But we all LEAVE at 3:30," someone complained.

"And my bank closes at 5:30," someone else added.

"You are hoping we'll all wait until Monday." The crowd was getting ugly.

"I'm sorry," Jerry held his hands up. "That's the way it has to be."

Jerry and Debbie turned and walked back down the hall followed by a shower of complaints, curses, and insults. Even Myrtle was furious. She was so upset she sounded like someone tapdancing on whoopie cushions.

June climbed on top of her desk and whistled. This succeeded in getting everyone quieted down, but now everyone was looking at her, expecting her to say something to fix the situation.

"Listen everybody, I will talk to Jerry as soon as I can. I'm just as unhappy about this as the rest of you. I promise. But I am unlikely to get him to change this back today. He is having some kind of cash issue and Debbie thinks this is a good idea. I hope I can get him to change his mind by next week. But I'm afraid I won't be able to do anything about this in the next few hours."

"Strike," hollered Dean sloppily.

June glared at him. "Don't be silly. Then we wouldn't get paid at all."

June did try to talk to Jerry that afternoon, but his arguments weren't even rational. He insisted there was a 'cash flow problem.' He would yell to Debbie, "How much do we have in the checking account?" She would yell back, "We are overdrawn."

June knew it was practically impossible, but if Jerry was burying all the profits under his house, who knew? Or worse, maybe it was all going up Jerry's nose. Or maybe it was a combination of both.

June told the group that, for the time being, they were going to have to deal with the new policy. She did promise them that she would try to find a bank that stayed open later so they could still deposit their checks on Friday evening.

A lot of Jerry's employees were people who couldn't afford to make waves. That allowed Jerry to get away with some pretty rotten behavior.

Not for the first time, June wondered if she should get

out. She also wondered if, like everybody else at Rock Shirt, she suffered from 'circumstances.' She didn't think so, but then, why did she stay? It had turned out better than she had initially expected, but there were a lot of times she didn't think she could put up with Jerry's crap any longer.

June and her posse went out for a few beers while they waited for 6:00. She was a little tipsy by the time Debbie handed her the pay envelope. June tore it open and whooped with joy. She knew at least one reason she stayed. She was making a lot of money these days. Sales had been increasing exponentially.

Debbie's smirk slipped and became a grimace.

Debbie makes out all the checks, so she knows what we all get in commission, June realized.

As she left for the weekend, June pointed at the plant that now engulfed half of Debbie's desk. "Don't let the plant get you," she told her.

CHAPTER 9

SATURDAY, AUGUST 6, 1988

Milwaukee was a beautiful place for June to be that summer. Her new apartment had a patio that overlooked a park. She had gotten control of her finances for the first time in her life, and she even opened a savings account.

She had a real bedroom, with a real bed and mattress. A futon in an efficiency apartment was an uncomfortable stop gap, but she had been living that way for two years. She finally felt like she was a functioning adult for the first time.

She was spending all of her time either at work or hanging out with people she worked with. So much so that her friend Kate was feeling terribly neglected.

June took advantage of a beautiful summer Saturday to invite Kate on a picnic at the county park near the zoo. June picked up Kate in the Shove-It.

"I can't believe you are still driving this thing," Kate

was appalled. She hung on as they hit a bumpy stretch of road with all the grace of an aged stripper grinding down the runway.

There was a loud bang and Kate screamed.

"Shit," June wrestled with the steering wheel. "I've blown a tire."

She managed to steer the car onto the soft shoulder. She waited for a break in traffic before she jumped out and slammed the door. She went around to the back and opened the hatch.

"Aren't you going to get out and help me?"

"No," Kate pouted.

"Fine," June snapped.

She opened the compartment that contained the spare tire. It wasn't a real tire; it was one of those little temporary tires. She also found both pieces of the jack and threw them on the ground before reclosing the hatch.

The handle of the jack was also a tire iron. She remembered to loosen the lug nuts before putting the jack under the rear bumper of the Chevette. She pumped the handle until the jack was fully extended, however her tire was still sitting flat on the ground. She smacked the handle, and the jack came down with a thump.

Kate got out and came around to the back of the car. "What's wrong?"

"I've got it now. I had to move the jack." June fussed with the jack until it was under the frame of the car. She pumped the handle again with the same result. The tire still refused to lift off the ground.

"You know," Kate began gently, "I don't know that much about cars, but I believe the top part and the bottom part should be attached to each other in some way."

"I think it's broken," June said stupidly.

"Whatever has happened, it can't be safe to drive around like that."

"What should I do?" June was drawing a complete blank. She felt utterly defeated. "Fucking Shove-It!" She kicked the tire and stubbed her toe, so she stomped up and down the side of the road swearing at the air.

"June," Kate scolded. "Pull yourself together. I think it's time this thing was put to sleep."

"It still runs," June stubbornly insisted.

"No. It. Don't. Think about its quality of life. Think about YOURS. And MINE!"

June knew Kate was right. The turn signal switch had recently snapped off in her hand. The horn didn't work. Neither did the windshield wipers, radio, or heat. About all it would do was start. At least she was making decent money. A couple more checks and she would be able to get a reliable car.

Kate took the bag with the picnic goodies out of the back seat and June removed the plate from the back of the Shove-It. Abandoning it seemed the only sensible solution.

Kate and June hiked a few blocks to an intersection. It had a gas station, so Kate went in and called a cab to take them back to Kate's.

They picnicked on Kate's living room floor and tried to catch up. It seemed to June that SO MUCH had happened to her since the beginning of the year, she couldn't possibly explain it all to Kate.

June spent the night on Kate's sofa, and then Kate drove her home after they had coffee and donuts and June heard about Kate's break-up with her latest boyfriend. He sounded like a real asshole; June was glad she never had to meet him.

CHAPTER 10

TUESDAY, OCTOBER4, 1988

The death of the Chevette didn't change June's life much. She took a bus to and from work, which was fine since she lived downtown, and her new apartment was on a bus route. But she was further isolated from people she didn't see at work.

She was spending almost all her free time with the secret society, as she had started calling them. She was not unhappy with her situation. She liked her job and the people she worked with, and June and Ann had become practically inseparable.

June's infatuation with Leo hadn't cooled, but they had become close friends. He told her about his family members in town, and he told her what it had been like growing up in a small village in Jamaica.

June's job was a snap. June had stopped trying to get

Jerry to delegate some of his authority, and instead had become accustomed to his pinball style of management. It amazed June that any work got done at all at Rock Shirt with the amount of goofing off that went on every day. June was finding herself in a very comfortable rut. It was hard to complain about getting paid so much for doing so little.

Jerry was deliriously happy these days, as long as the sales and money kept pouring in. The biggest problem was still keeping shirts in stock, but Jerry handled all such details personally. They had completely given up on the idea of adding an extra phone shift because they were overloaded with orders as it was.

June trained the occasional new employee and acted as the go-between for the phone people and Jerry. Customer complaints were rare, and Jerry – or rather, Jack Snow – dealt with all of them personally.

Jerry actually encouraged his employees to goof off. He was constantly throwing impromptu parties during working hours. A staff birthday often meant that no work got done that day.

June faced a new problem with keeping the phone people working. They had called all the available record stores, and then t-shirt shops. They had also gone through all the variety stores, gift shops and arcades.

She was running out of lists to purchase for cold calling, but with the stock problems it hardly mattered. They were currently trying to sell to head shops, but the list company didn't differentiate between head shops and tobacconists. Tobacconists were winning nine to one, and the phone people were finding it very tedious to be constantly told no.

June was wallowing in complacency, with her feet up

on her desk, when Sharon approached with a pained expression on her face. "What's wrong, Sharon. You look upset."

"It's Jerry," Sharon started. It looked like she might cry.

June jumped out of her chair. "Oh my God. What did he do to you?" June realized she was squeezing Sharon's arm too tightly.

"He keeps grabbing my ass. I told him to stop it, but he won't."

June's fear turned to red hot rage. "You DO NOT have to take that."

"What if he fires me?"

"He wouldn't dare," June promised. "I'm glad you told me. I'll take care of it."

"Don't get me fired."

"Are you kidding? I'm going to get you a raise." June smiled, "He won't touch you again."

The door to Jerry's office was closed. Debbie looked up from her desk as June stomped into the outer office. "You can't go in there. Jerry's in a meeting with his lawyer."

"Good." June walked right in and slammed the door behind her. "Hello, Monty. I'm glad you're here."

Monty looked startled but didn't say anything.

June gave Jerry a look that implied he was less attractive than a grease trap. "Jerry, we need to have a serious discussion."

"June, you can't…"

"Jerry, you're a pig. You stay the hell away from Sharon."

"June, I didn't…"

"It's bad enough you bring prostitutes in here. I can't believe you tried to set that one up last week working in the packing room!"

"I was just trying to help her out."

"You're so full of shit!"

"I was joking around with Sharon."

"She doesn't think it's funny, and neither do I." June stormed out and slammed the door hard enough to knock a picture off the wall.

"This is worse than when you bootlegged those AIDS charity shirts," Monty sniffed.

Later that day, June was sitting at her desk when Jerry came into the phone room with new shirts to sell. "ATTENTION, you can now sell Hell Beasts, Girls on Sheep, and Children of the Purple Night."

He dumped the shirts on June's desk and smiled contritely. "Where's Sharon?" he asked.

"She went home sick."

Jerry nodded and turned to walk away.

"Don't you think you should call her and apologize?" June called after him.

"Yeah, I know…"

"AND give her a raise."

"HEY. I never even touched her."

"That's not what she says."

There was a commotion in the outer hall. Suddenly, Virgil burst into the phone room. "IT'S A RAID," he yelled to Jerry. "The Feds are in the print room."

"It's been nice knowing you," said Cliff as he ran past them carrying his briefcase.

A half dozen phone people stared at Jerry, waiting for instructions. "Take all your file boxes and scatter. We don't want them taking our client lists. Split up so they can't follow you. Get out and go home. We'll call you and tell you when it's safe to come back."

Then he turned to June. "Lock the door and then go."

Jerry ran down the inner hall and back to his office. June held the outer door open for the phone people and then watched them scatter before locking the door. June was wishing she had planned something for this eventuality.

She looked out of the windows down to the street. There were several blue FBI vans parked around the front entrance of the building, but it didn't look like they were watching any of the other exits. There were many businesses on all floors of the old warehouse, so they weren't stopping people from leaving. That was a relief.

June ran to the front and found the outer office filled with cops wearing blue bullet-proof vests and carrying rifles. They were tearing up the office and carrying out the drawers full of files from the cabinets. Jerry was trying to stop them by inserting himself between the officers and the files.

June wondered where Debbie was, but only for a second. She was sure Jerry had told her to get out with the books as soon as Virgil raised the alarm.

"You can't take EVERYTHING," Jerry protested. "It says you're only supposed to take records that pertain to the sale of Summerland licensed designs," he read from some papers he was crushing. "That's what it says on the complaint." Jerry grabbed and hung onto the filing cabinet.

One of the cops with a clip board and a walkie-talkie addressed Jerry. "Obviously we are NOT going through everything piece by piece right now. Someone will do that later. The rest of the material will be returned to you when we are finished with it."

Jerry groaned and opened his mouth to protest.

"We are taking the files, Mr. Cooper, so get out of the way or you will be arrested."

Jerry got out of the way.

"Did you call Monty?" June asked Jerry.

"I thought I told you to go." Jerry replied.

"Okay, but did you?"

"What is your name, Miss?" An agent and a gun stepped between June and Jerry.

"I don't have to tell you that," June tried to seem NOT completely freaked out.

"I'm afraid you do."

Jerry was winking and shaking his head and trying to signal her not to say anything.

"Smith," she finally answered.

"Can I see some identification?"

"I left my ID in my other spacesuit."

The agent slowly frowned. June thought better of it and made a run for it down the inner hall. He wasn't really interested in arresting her; he wanted her to stop talking to Jerry.

She ended up in the packing room where many cops were stuffing shirts into boxes to be carried out. June approached a cop that looked like he was in charge, because he wasn't really doing anything.

"What designs are you supposed to take?" she asked in a businesslike tone.

"Here's the complaint," he shoved a stapled packet of papers at her without looking in her direction.

June looked over the complaint and the list of Summerland designs. There were a lot of bands on the list

– twenty or so – including all of their most popular classic rock shirts. She sighed.

Cops were everywhere loading shirts into boxes and sealing them up with packing tape. June noticed one of the cops loading the latest Hell Beasts shirts into a box. She doubled-checked the list to be sure, but she KNEW that band wasn't one of the ones in the complaint.

"HEY! Not those," June hollered loudly. "Put those back."

"Oops. My mistake," he said and made a run for it out of the packing room. It would have been more convincing if he didn't have one sticking out of his blue vest.

"CROOKED!" June screamed after him.

She then quietly unpacked the box and put the shirts back on the shelf. An icy sleet started to fall, spattering the dirty windows.

She always knew cops were only as honest as the general population, and that wasn't too good, but it scared her to think they were both corruptible and heavily armed.

Since she had started working at Rock Shirt, June felt like she had been walking a moral tightrope. She didn't like all the rationalizing she had been doing to justify her behavior and the actions of her friends.

She was also worried that Jerry and Debbie were up to something that could get her into trouble, something a lot worse than copyright infringement.

CHAPTER 11

WEDNESDAY, OCTOBER 5, 1988

June hesitated as she entered the front office the next morning. She was expecting a big mess, but the place was just sort of empty and quiet.

Debbie came out of Jerry's office and seemed startled to see June standing there. "Oh, hello," Debbie said.

"Is Jerry here?"

"He's in his office talking to Monty."

June knocked lightly on the door before walking in. "How is everything?" she asked the pair.

"Everything is fine," Jerry's joviality was obviously forced. "Call all of your people and tell them they can come back to work."

"What are they supposed to sell?"

"Everything except the Summerland stuff. It's fine.

Just carry on as normal."

June looked at Monty, but he was staring at some papers on Jerry's desk to avoid looking in her direction. He looked unshowered and hung-over.

June went to her desk and started calling all the phone people. She told them to come back, but with caution. If they saw any police vehicles or FBI vans, they should turn back around.

She hung up the phone and leaned back in her chair. The room looked empty, but otherwise unchanged. *Funny*, June thought, *it didn't feel the same.*

By lunchtime, almost everyone was back at their desks, even if it seemed like some of them had come back only out of morbid curiosity.

Because they had all hung onto their little index boxes, they still had all their client contacts, and they spent the afternoon calling their biggest customers and assuring them they would still be getting most of what they wanted.

Jerry was taking the whole thing in stride, at least he was pretending very well. He insisted sales would be back to normal in a week.

June was pleased to see that Sharon had come back to work. "Did you get a raise?" June asked her.

Sharon chuckled. "I got a good bonus."

June grinned at her and patted her back just as Virgil burst into the phone room. June experienced a flash of déjà vu.

"News reporters are here," Virgil yelled. "Lock yourselves in and be quiet."

June jumped up and locked the door behind him. Everyone else ran to the windows and looked down to the street.

"All the channels have satellite vans parked across the

street," Cliff hissed. He did not look the least bit comfortable. "I'm getting out."

"Wait" Leo called him back. "Hold this up as you leave," he said as he handed Cliff a shirt that said, Fuck the System.

June shushed everyone and listened at the door. She could hear a woman knocking on one of the doors a little further up the hallway.

"Anybody else want to get out now?" she asked the room. Several others, including Myrtle, decided to go also.

"Ready?" she asked them, and they all nodded. They each held a rude shirt at the ready and hustled through the doorway before June closed and locked the door behind them.

Right away they could hear shouts from the news people as the phone people scattered into the building. Then they heard the TV people come back down the hallway before there was a very loud knock on the phone room door.

Everybody froze. June put a finger up to her lips and prayed they would go away and give up. More pounding. The people that were left were all staring at June for instructions. She had to fight the urge to laugh.

Suddenly, the TV people all started running back up the hallway to the front office. The people up there had taken the opportunity the phone people had provided to make an escape of their own.

Now they were pounding on the front office door, and everyone could hear one of the reporters yelling, "We know you're in there, Mr. Cooper. We saw your face pressed up against the glass."

They had been waiting for a painfully long time when Sharon said, "I've got to pee."

"So do I," said Ann earnestly.

June groaned. "We should all try to get out together. I don't think those reporters are going to give up for a while." Everyone bunched together near the door.

Ann said, "We should meet outside the bathrooms on the fourth floor."

"I'm going home," Katrina said. She was a newer employee. June wondered if she'd come back tomorrow.

"You can go if you want to. Be careful coming in tomorrow morning, everybody," June warned. "Okay, scatter."

June opened the door, and everyone ran for it. They split up at the stairwell, and the press people were not in the mood for a wild goose chase on stairs. June made it to the fourth floor about the time they were all getting there.

"That was surprisingly simple," Charlie said. "I don't think they bothered to chase us."

"What do we do now?" Sharon asked.

"Let's take off and get something to eat," Ann said.

"And some beer," Charlie added.

"You guys take off," June decided. "I'm going to wait for a while and then try to get back in the office. I am getting pretty fucking sick of this. I might have to just march in there and let them take my picture."

"See you tomorrow… I hope!" Ann laughed as the gang headed towards the freight cage, everybody but Leo.

June leaned against the wall. "You going too?"

"I want to show you something."

June raised an eyebrow.

"Follow me," Leo laughed. He went to the end of the hall and turned the corner into a dead end.

"Leo? What the…"

"Up you go."

There was a ladder bolted to the wall that went up to a trapdoor in the ceiling.

"You have GOT to be kidding. What's up there?"

"The roof."

"No way." June protested.

"I'll be right behind you."

June was not sure about this at all. This was an old crumbly building. She didn't want to die falling from a rickety ladder at Rock Shirt.

Climbing up wasn't all that difficult. The trap door led to a little shack that housed the motors for the freight elevator. There was a door in the wall that led out to the roof – an enormous expanse of tarpaper and gravel.

Leo was right behind her and led her to the edge. "Check out de view."

The icy rain of the previous day was long gone. The sun was shining brightly, and the air was crisp and the wind cool. Fallen leaves skittered across the tarpaper making a scratching sound.

The city doesn't look too bad from up here. June looked at Leo. *He doesn't look bad either*.

He was about an inch shorter than June, and his glasses made him look bookish. Behind his glasses, his eyes were like melted chocolate, and his smile lit up his face like a bonfire.

"Leo," June moved closer to him. "Why do you work for Jerry?"

"What do you mean?" Leo looked serious.

"Virgil told me that everyone who works for Jerry has extenuating circumstances, some skeleton in their closet that keeps them here. I didn't believe him at the time."

"But now you are not sure?"

"Leo, do you have circumstances?"

"Yes." Leo looked at June for a long time before he continued. "I don't have a green card, so Jerry pays me in cash."

June's heart fell into her stomach with a splash.

"What about you? Why do you work for Jerry?" he asked her.

It was a fair question, one that she had been thinking about a lot lately. She still didn't have a good answer. "Because no one in their right mind would do it for free."

"No jokes now," he protested. "I am being very serious. You must have some reason. You aren't the kind to put up wit his shit just for da money."

"Part of it is the money," June admitted. "But it's more than that."

"You like him."

"Who?"

"Jerry. You like him," Leo insisted.

"He's a slimeball."

"Yes, but a likable slimeball. I like him too! Most of da time."

"I like my job," June tried to explain to herself as well as to Leo. "It's the least awful one I've ever had."

"Look!" Leo pointed down to the street suddenly. "The reporters are leaving."

One of the reporters looked up and spotted June and Leo on the roof and pointed them out.

Leo and June waved back. "Good-bye!"

CHAPTER 12

FRIDAY, OCTOBER 7, 1988

Friday at Rock Shirt seemed to drag on endlessly, like a 5-hour baby shower for a distant cousin. June needed to talk to SOMEONE she didn't work with.

She called Kate and invited her to meet her at Rock Shirt at 3:30. They were going out for happy hour and await the witching hour, otherwise known as Jerry's 6:00 payroll disbursement.

It had been a rough week. The bust had seriously disrupted business and scared off a lot of customers. Nine people had quit, and five of those were phone people. On the bright side, one of them was Cliff. The same old crew was still around, but then, they had nowhere else to go.

Jerry was still optimistic. He insisted things would get back to normal quickly, but he was spending a lot of time on the phone trying to reassure customers. June was spending a lot of time trying to reassure herself.

The day before, Leo hadn't turned up for work, and he hadn't called in either. June was badly shaken. She had been pretending she wasn't attracted to him for months now, but all that practice hadn't improved her performance. She was hoping he would still show up with a good excuse and a funny story, but she didn't really believe it would happen.

The weather had turned cold and windy again. The leaves were changing from yellow and orange to brown, blowing from the trees in the bitter breeze.

"My customer is demanding to speak to Jack Snow!" Myrtle broke into June's thoughts.

June had been staring into her half cup of cold coffee. She snapped out of it. "Take his number and I'll have Jerry call him back."

June had expected Myrtle to quit. She had lost several good customers and a lot of commission. Surprisingly, she wasn't upset by either the bust or the media attention. She got a kick out of it. But money was the reason Myrtle worked at Rock Shirt and June wasn't sure how long she would stay.

June got the number from Myrtle and took it to Jerry in his office. He was just coming out with a young woman.

"June," Jerry started, "this is Laura. She'll be starting on the phones Monday."

"Nice to meet you," June stuck out her hand.

"Good-bye," said Laura flatly and walked out without returning the handshake.

"She was just leaving," Jerry explained feebly.

"Where did you find her?" June gestured to the closing door.

"I met her yesterday when I went to visit Beth."

"Where IS Beth?"

"She's in the hospital."

"What's wrong?"

Jerry scratched his beard and looked up at the ceiling. "I can't remember. I mean, they're not sure."

"You are a TERRIBLE liar, Jerry," June laughed. "Why don't you want to tell me? Surely by now you know you can trust me."

"Yeah," Jerry said with sudden sincerity. "You always did shoot pretty straight."

"Yardsticks, you mean?"

Jerry paused, but only for a split second. "She tried to kill herself. She's in County."

"My GOD! Is she alright?"

"She'll be okay."

"What happened? Why? What's going on?" June was angry but she didn't know where to focus it..

"I don't know." Jerry just shook his head.

"Wait a minute." June suddenly realized something. "You hired somebody you met out at County? Was she visiting someone?"

"No, she was a patient. She didn't escape or anything. They let her out yesterday."

June should have been surprised, but it was typical of Jerry. He liked to hire people that would be indebted to him, no matter how damaged they might be. The fact she was young and attractive Jerry would consider a big plus.

June handed Jerry the message from Myrtle's customer. "Another complaint for Jack Snow."

Just then Kate came in the door from the outer corridor. "Hurray! I can't believe I found this place. It's worse than a hedge maze."

"Who's you friend?" Jerry smiled saccharinely and

kissed Kate's hand.

June thought she might gag. Instead she rolled her eyes. "Jerry, Kate. Kate, Jerry. Come on, Kate. I'll give you the tour."

"Nice boss," Kate giggled when they were out of earshot. "I like his suit."

Naturally, Kate had heard stories about Rock Shirt and its band of wackos, but she was still impressed by the genuine strangeness of the place.

After the tour they went to La Bourgeoise for wine and cheese. The café was empty at that time of the afternoon.

It was a half floor below street level in one of the old buildings in the Third Ward. Inside, it had brick walls and high windows full of hanging plants. There was a service counter near the door for carry-outs.

The dining area was too full of intimate little wrought iron tables with matching little wrought iron chairs that were very trendy. The floor of the café was flagstone, so every table and every chair wobbled badly. June didn't much care for the food, which was also very trendy, but you can't go wrong with cheese and wine.

June hadn't eaten all day, so after two glasses of wine she was already spilling her guts to Kate. In a nutshell, June loved and hated her job simultaneously. One of the main reasons she loved her job may have just quit, which was just as well since she didn't want him anyway.

"Why not," Kate asked.

"I'm his boss," June explained.

"So?"

"I can't ask out one of my employees! It doesn't look like he's ever going to ask me out. Anyway, I'll probably never see him again." June felt like crying so she took a huge gulp of wine and ended up choking herself.

Kate patted June on the back. When June finally stopped coughing, Kate said, "Come on. It's after 6:00. Let's go get your check; then we'll go out to dinner and a club, hey?"

When they got to the office there were several other people there picking up checks as well. They squeezed into the crowded room and June saw Leo standing near the doorway to Jerry's office.

"Leo!" June's face gave her away. Damn that French wine.

Kate looked amused. "Aren't you going to introduce me to your friend?"

"Kate, Leo. Leo Kate," she blurted quickly before turning her back on Kate to look Leo in the eyes. "Are you alright," she asked intensely.

"I'm fine," he assured her. "I just come to git paid."

"Did you quit?" She tried not to sound completely freaked out.

"No, I just won't be working for a while." He took her hand, and they went down the hallway followed by 18 eyes. She hoped they were far enough away from 18 ears.

Leo lowered his voice so they wouldn't get most of it. "Dey deport my brother! Him wife had to leave for Jamaica today. Dey won't let him apply to come back for 5 years now."

He was very upset, and June noticed his accent got stronger when he was stressed. It was a very bad sign, so she tried not to enjoy it. "What are you going to do?" She was afraid of the answer, but she asked anyway.

"I can't help him, but I am helping the rest of my family move to Chicago. Den I come back 'ere."

"How long will you be gone?" Damn the wine. She

sounded grief stricken.

"I don't know," he shrugged.

June completely embarrassed herself by bursting into tears. Leo pulled her into a hug, and she sobbed into his shirt.

"I really like you, June," he told her, "but you do not want to git involved wit me right now. Anyway, I'm not your type."

June wiped her face on her sleeve. "How do you know what my type is?"

Leo shook his head and laughed. "I'll see you when I git back."

Leo went back to the front office. June hung back and attempted to compose herself. She went to the restroom and washed her face and combed her hair. She looked almost human, so she went back to collect Kate and her check.

Nobody was in the outer office. They had all gotten their pay and fled. June could hear Kate talking to Jerry in his office, so she walked in.

June was not in the mood for surprises. It took her about 5 seconds before she registered what was going on. Jerry, Debbie, and Kate were standing around Jerry's desk, and Debbie was snorting an enormous line of cocaine from the photo of the DeLorean, which now lay on Jerry's desk. Kate was playing with her nose and sniffing.

Debbie straightened up and handed a rolled up bill to June.

"No thanks," June waved it off. "Let's go, Kate."

"Party pooper," Debbie called her.

"Thanks for the hospitality," Kate told Jerry and kissed him on the cheek.

June wanted to puke.

Once they were in the elevator, June let Kate have it. "I can't believe it. I leave you alone for 5 minutes, and when I get back you're doing lines with my BOSS?"

"He's not so bad once you get to know him."

"WRONG. He is really horrible when you get to know him. Take my word for that."

"Tell me about the other guy," Kate artfully changed the subject. "The guy you like."

"Leo," June sighed.

"Right. I didn't know you had a thing for black guys."

June was offended. "I DON'T! I mean…not necessarily."

"Okay, okay. Don't get mad," Kate laughed. "I think he's cute. REALLY."

"God, you're obnoxious when you're high. Where do you want to go for dinner?"

"Well…" Kate scoffed, "I'm not very hungry. NOW."

"Great. It figures."

CHAPTER 13

THURSDAY, NOVEMBER 3, 1988

Jane waded through the auto ads in the newspaper with her feet up on her desk. She had been trying to find a used car for months, and she was beginning to feel funny about it.

Her fussiness had more to do with the ultimatum she had given herself than with any real difficulty she had finding a reliable vehicle. June had promised herself that once she found a car, she would start looking for a more stable job.

She had saved plenty of money. After the Summerland bust, sales had gone down for a couple of weeks, but then they started going up again. About a month after the bust, sales were almost what they were the week before it.

Leo had not returned to Rock Shirt. She had heard a rumor recently from Peg in the print room that he was back in town, but she didn't have confirmation. She didn't know if it was true, and she was afraid to find out, so she tried not to think about it.

A few other people had quit. Myrtle had gotten a job in an insurance office and gleefully waved good-bye to everyone. Jerry was continually hiring new people to replace the ones that left. He was finding it hard to keep all the phones filled, but it was just as well.

June was running out of ideas for calling potential new customers. They were now trying toy stores, roller rinks, and amusement parks. Slim pickings to be sure. June thought they could start at the beginning and call records stores again once a year had passed. She would have to order it ahead of time and then try to mark out all the stores that were already ordering from Rock Shirt.

Jerry did not agree that they should wait a year. He pushed June to come up with new ways of expanding. He constantly complained about 'cash flow,' and invented new schemes to take in money faster and pay it out slower.

He even asked June to investigate the exchange rate for various European currencies, but so far June had been able to talk him out of expanding overseas. Even the vague promise of a trip to Europe wasn't enough to make her supportive of his scheme.

She didn't know how long it would be before Jerry's greed over-rode his common sense. She even tried to talk to him about going straight, and attempting to get contracts for licensed designs, but he had no interest in it. He insisted the business moved too fast. He was always chasing the hottest thing, and nothing stayed hot for very long.

June was consistently amazed at how easy the shirts were to sell, but there were limits to how much sales could expand. Jerry seemed to believe sales should keep increasing exponentially. He started insisting the phone people make several hours of cold calls a day.

It was frustrating for people to be told to call dozens of unsuitable businesses to find one that they could even try, so June shouldn't have been too shocked when Jerry picked up one of the extensions in the office and heard a phone-in sex line.

"WHO'S ON THIS PHONE?" Everyone could hear him bellow from the front office. He then came stampeding into the phone room. He slammed the door and threw himself in front of it. "Nobody is leaving this room until I find out which one of you was on that line!"

June put down her newspaper and jumped up from her desk. She ran over to him and asked, "What the hell are you on about?"

"Someone is using these phones to have phone sex!"

June stifled a laugh. "How do you know?"

"I just heard it in the office. One of these phone lines is connected to one of the lines on the office phone."

"Well, there are only three new phones. Who was using them," June asked the group. They were all shifting from one foot to the other and looking at the floor. The silence was VERY uncomfortable to everyone.

"Wait," someone finally said. "I confess." He stepped forward.

It was Mike, a newish employee. He was about 18 and one of the better salespeople. He was smart and had a good sense of humor. Everybody liked him. June tried to keep a smirk off her face.

"You're fired." Jerry pointed at Mike's chest. The smirk slid off June's face. Then Jerry spoke to the rest of the group. "Get back to work. We will talk about this later." He opened the door and stomped back to his office.

June finally let out the breath she had been holding. Everyone looked at June, waiting for her to fix it.

She rolled her eyes. "I'll go talk to him. I just want to give him a few minutes to calm down. Mike, you should take off for today. Call me in the morning. Okay you guys, back to the phones, and try to actually do some work for the rest of the afternoon," June scolded.

Nobody was the least bit intimidated by June. She had no real authority. Ugh. What a shit job this was turning out to be today.

After a brief cooling off period, June went to talk to Jerry. Debbie was standing on guard outside the big door.

"You can't go in there," Debbie told June. "He's pissed off. You do not want to go in there."

"Debbie, why don't you mind your own business for once?" June attempted to push past her, but Debbie stood her ground. Debbie put her hand on June's shoulder and gave her a shove, causing June to almost fall over backwards.

June's eyes flashed as she thought of several violent things she could do to Debbie.

"It's about time Jerry fired one of you PHONE PEOPLE," Debbie said with unveiled disgust. "You all get paid loads of money to sit around and goof off," she snarled.

June swallowed hard. "The people in that room are my responsibility. Where do you get off commenting on the way we do our jobs? It has nothing to do with you. Just because you make out the payroll doesn't mean you get a say in what people get paid."

"I keep the books. That means I have an obligation to speak up if company money is being wasted."

"We are not paid hourly, Debbie. They only get paid a LOT of money when they MAKE a lot of sales for the company. They happen to be very good at sales, so they deserve the commission they make. You can keep your sour grapes to yourself."

June spun around and stomped back to the phone room. Her fight with Jerry would have to wait. When she entered the phone room, everyone looked at her expectantly, but she just shook her head. She would talk to Jerry about Mike when he was in a better mood, and when Debbie wasn't hanging around.

Several people confessed to June that Mike wasn't the only one that had been wasting time on the phones. People had been calling horoscope hotlines and all different kinds of phone services for at least a month. June called the phone company and found out that they were paying a flat rate for time spent on any call, but they were not being charged the huge fees normally associated with 900 numbers.

Unfortunately, the three new lines that had been put in, connected to the general office lines for the business, and would be charged the per-minute rate. There was a big bill on the way, and June figured she better warn Jerry about it before it arrived in the mail.

June told the crew in no uncertain terms to knock it off. She also said that they would no longer be required to spend a specified amount of time making cold calls each day.

After everyone had left for the day, June was still at her desk doing paperwork. She decided to hang around and talk to Jerry after Debbie had gone home. She wasn't on commission, so she normally worked until 5:00.

At 4:30 Ann tossed an order on June's desk with a

heavy sigh. "That's it. Let's blow this place."

"Not yet. I've still got to talk to Jerry about Mike."

"Well, hurry up. I want to see The Twinkies. They're playing tonight at Harpo's."

Before June could reply, Sharon came in from the outer hallway. "Let's go, we'll miss the bus!"

"Can't we catch the next one," June asked. "I really want to wait until 'you-know-who' goes home."

"Who?" Sharon looked puzzled, but then, Sharon always looked puzzled.

"Talk to him now," Ann insisted.

"Talk to who," Sharon asked.

"JERRY," June and Ann said simultaneously.

"Yes?" Jerry heard his name and stuck his head in the phone room doorway.

"Can we talk? In your office," June asked.

"Sorry. Have to do it tomorrow. I'm on my way out." Jerry's head disappeared.

"Jerry, wait." June tried to follow him and ran out into the hall.

Jerry's retreating figure gave her that dismissive wave that she was really starting to loath.

"Shit."

Ann and Sharon joined her in the hall. "We may as well try to catch the bus," Ann said.

The three women had to run for it, but they managed to catch the number 15 bus. It was rush hour, which meant it was standing room only. June enjoyed standing up on a moving bus. It was kind of like surfing. But she didn't like it when everyone was crushed together like cigarettes in a pack.

They got off the bus at Brady Street and Prospect

Avenue. It was still early, and Sharon wanted to get something to eat. They decided to grab a sub sandwich at Cousins' despite Ann's insistence that they hurry.

As they grabbed a table and sat down to eat their sandwiches, June asked, "How come you're in such a hurry, Ann. Bands usually don't start until 9:00."

"Yeah," Sharon agreed. "You haven't told us nothin'. We don't even know what band we are going to see."

Ann paused to swallow a huge bite of cheesesteak. "I want to see The Twinkies." They're opening for another band, so they are supposed to start around 8:00."

"Oh man," Sharon spewed shredded lettuce all over the table. "We have LOADS of time. What's the rush?"

Ann fiddled with her sandwich. "I'd just like to get there a bit early, is all."

"Ann, you are being very suspicious. What have you got cooked up for tonight?" June asked.

Ann sighed and put down the rest of her sandwich. "Okay. Okay, I like a guy in the band, alright?"

"Why didn't you just say so?" June asked. "So, what kind of music do these twinkies play?"

"I'm not sure," Ann reluctantly admitted, "but they are opening for Yakkin Travis and the Reggae All Stars."

"Reggae is good." Sharon mumbled through a mouthful of sandwich.

"Where did you meet this guy," June asked.

"He works at the record store by my building. He is SO cute," Ann gushed. "He's 6 foot 4 and has long, blonde, heavy-metal hair!"

June took a big bite of her sandwich to stop herself from laughing.

When they finished, they walked over to Harpo's Bar. It was cold and flurries swirled around them as they hurried along the uneven sidewalk. The bar was still empty. They hadn't yet started collecting the cover charge at the door. A couple of stringy looking guys were on the dark stage messing with wiring and setting up speakers.

"There he is," Ann whispered loudly.

"Which one," June asked.

"The one in the ripped t-shirt," Ann replied.

"What's his name," Sharon asked.

"Thor."

"Thor?" June and Sharon said together.

"Jinx!" Ann laughed.

June's eyes had finally adjusted to the dim lighting, so she checked out the guys on the stage. One had a huge haystack of hair dyed jet black. The other guy had a huge haystack of hair bleached platinum blonde. The blonde one had to be Thor. June thought he looked like a drought-stricken cornstalk.

"What'll it be, ladies?" the bartender said flatly.

"I'll get a pitcher." June volunteered, handing the man a 20. "Miller," she told him.

"Well, go say hi," Sharon told Ann.

"No way. Not yet," Ann answered. "I'm playing it cool. He's bound to notice us and come over. There's hardly anybody here."

"I don't know. It's pretty dark in here," June commented.

He looks pretty busy." Ann was making excuses.

"Go on!" Sharon insisted. "Just say hello."

"Oh, all right." Ann gathered her courage and inched her way slowly towards the stage.

"What an unlikely couple." June said to Sharon. "He's more than a foot taller than she is."

"They say opposites attract," Sharon philosophized.

"I never used to believe that," June replied.

June and Sharon had finished the pitcher by the time Ann came back to the table. "He wants me to hang around until after they finish their set," she bubbled.

"That's great!" Sharon patted Ann on the back.

The Twinkies began the show with a shriek of feedback and a scream; "WE ARE THE TWINKIES!" They launched into a guitar torturing demonstration, while a chunky guy with a shaved head beat himself against a set of drums.

June excused herself with hand signals. She went into the ladies' room and stuffed some toilet paper into her ears. She fixed her hair and make-up, but eventually she had to go back to the table. When she got back, they were halfway through another song, which sounded exactly like the first song except Thor was screaming some pornographic lyrics.

Someone had bought another pitcher of beer, and June helped herself. Beer seemed to make the band sound better, so she had some more. The Twinkies played a short set of 6 songs, but by the time they were finished, June was completely stewed.

After a short break, Thor joined the three ladies, and the reggae band started their set. They were very good. June was having fun for a change. She surreptitiously removed her earplugs and leaned back in her chair. This was not bad at all.

CHAPTER 14

FRIDAY, NOVEMBER 4, 1988

When the band finished their set Sharon stood up. "I've got to get home. See you guys tomorrow." She headed for the door before stopping and coming back to the table. "HEY, isn't that Leo over there by the door?"

June spun around and spotted Leo instantly. He was sitting at a table with a group of friends. The young black woman next to him put her arm around him, and June spun back around. Her face turned red hot, and she wished she hadn't drunk so much beer.

"LEO," Sharon called to him and waved. June wished she could vanish, or dissolve. Anything to not be in this spot right now.

"Hello Sharon!" June heard Leo's familiar voice. He was coming over to their table. There was nowhere to hide. She hoped she didn't throw up.

Ann waved, "Hi, Leo."

June was trying to get control of her face. She felt a hand on her shoulder and Leo said, "Hello, June. I can't believe YOU'RE still at Rock Shirt." He sounded so disappointed. Disappointed in her.

She tried her best to smile but it came out more of a grimace.

Leo's date walked up behind him and slipped her arm through his. She smiled at all of them, waiting to be introduced.

"Dis is Tina," he said and made the introductions. She started pulling him back towards their friends. "Well, it was nice to see you again," Leo made his excuses. He looked at June, but she was studying her glass and wishing a sinkhole would open and swallow her whole.

After they walked away, June told Thor and Ann, "I better get going too. You two have a great night. See you tomorrow, Ann."

June grabbed her bag and bolted past Leo's table and out the door. The tears started as soon as her feet hit the sidewalk. She walked the couple of blocks to the lakefront. She found a park bench facing the water and sat down for a good cry.

She had thought Leo would have called her when he got back to town. She figured that was what had upset her so much. It wasn't like she had a reason to be crying her eyes out over him. He just caught her off guard. That was it.

She should be relieved, she told herself. At least she could stop thinking about him and wondering when he might turn up. At least she had stopped crying, and the cold night air off the lake helped her to sober up.

She looked at her watch and swore. It was too late for

her to take a bus home. She was only about a half a mile from Rock Shirt, so she decided to walk that way. She could let herself into the phone room and sleep on her desk. It was too bad she didn't have the key for the front office, or she could sleep on the couch.

She made her way to the 3rd floor up one of the back staircases and unlocked the phone room door. It was dark, but the streetlights shone in the greasy windows and made long strange shadows across the floor. She took the stuff off her desk and piled it on the floor. Grabbing a pile of t-shirts for a pillow, June tried to get comfortable and fall asleep.

June wasn't sure how long she had been asleep. It seemed like she had just dozed off when she heard voices in the hallway. She was suddenly wide awake. She rolled quickly off the desk and onto the floor. She wedged herself into the kneehole of her desk and held her breath.

"What was that?" She heard a man say.

"I didn't hear anything." June recognized Jerry's voice.

"It came from in there," said the other voice.

"It's not locked," Jerry said with surprise. "HELLO, anybody here?"

June probably should have said something, but she was completely frozen with fear.

"What was it," the voice asked. They came into the darkened room. June thought for sure they would be able to hear her heart beating.

"Some stuff fell off the desk, that's all. Nobody's here." June could see the men's legs from under the desk. They finally left and shut the door behind them.

June crawled out from under the desk. She ran on tiptoe over to the door and pressed her ear against it. She could hear them down the hall unlocking and entering the packing room.

She opened the door as quietly as she could and sneaked down the hall. Light was streaming from around the packing room door into the dark corridor. June peeked in and saw the back of Jerry's suit. He moved to one side and June could finally see the other man.

It was Debbie's husband, Chip. What were they doing here in the middle of the night?

June could only see a thin sliver of the room from this perspective, but she could see them re-opening several boxes that had already been packed with shirts and labeled for delivery by the packing crew. Chip had a gym bag that he unzipped. June watched him remove several small packages wrapped in white paper. They added a package to each of the boxes they had opened, and then resealed them all with shipping tape.

June tore herself away from the door. She scooted down the hall away from the Rock Shirt part of the third floor and around the corner, just as the packing room door opened and the men came out.

"Tell your wife she better be at work tomorrow morning, or I'll know why," Jerry joked. She could hear them shutting and locking the double-door on the packing room before they moved down the hall away from June.

"I still think I heard something before," Chip said. "Are you sure none of the other companies in this building run a third shift?"

"There's nobody here. I told you…" Jerry stopped short. "I thought I locked this door."

"You did. I saw you!" Chip's voice rose an octave. "I told you someone was in there."

"Nobody's in there." Jerry argued. "Look for yourself.

The lock is just broken; that's all. I'll have to have Virgil fix it."

June stood in the hallway for a long time after the voices faded down the corridor. She felt like the gears were slipping in her brain. Suddenly, she jumped into action.

Forgetting to be quiet, she ran back to the phone room and started rummaging around in the bottom drawer of her desk. She kept a few tools for repairing chairs and hanging shirts. She found a large screwdriver and a small hammer.

The packing room doors were big and loose, like a barn door. Each door had two widely spaced hinges on the outside of the door. June put the screwdriver against the top on the lower hinge and hit it up with the hammer.

The pin came loose and slid up. A few more smacks with the hammer and June could pull out the hinge pin. She could now pull the bottom of the door away from the doorframe wide enough for her to squeeze through.

She hit the light switch and temporarily blinded herself. She was going to have a nasty headache in the morning. She studied the pile of boxes, trying to identify the ones she thought had been tampered with. She grabbed an exacto-knife and a roll of tape.

She opened and reclosed three boxes before she found what she was looking for. It was 5:00 am and the sky was pink. The box with the packet in it was addressed to a record store in Oshkosh. June took the packet and stuffed it under her shirt, before closing the box and retaping it. She did her best to put everything back the way she had found it.

She turned out the lights, and replaced the pin in the hinge, which turned out to be the worst job of the night, but she finally did it.

She went back to the phone room and returned the tools to her desk. She put the packet in her purse but left the phone room the way Jerry had seen it, with the door unlocked.

Her brain was on autopilot as she walked down Water Street towards downtown. It wasn't until she was hiding behind a menu at George Webb's Hamburger Parlor that she felt she could breathe. Her waitress was a very wrinkly woman with big feet. She called June 'Honey' when she brought her scrambled eggs. She called everyone Honey.

What had June gotten herself into? Why did she do what she did? What was she supposed to do now? She took the packet because she wanted to have it when she confronted Jerry.

There was no way he could deny what he was up to if she had the proof in her hands, proof that could get her into terrible trouble, she realized. She really hadn't thought this whole thing through.

June was hungrier than she realized and quickly ate her eggs and drank three cups of coffee. She left the money and tip on the table before going to the back to use the restroom. June locked the door and set her purse in the sink. She took the paper packet out of her purse.

Taking a deep breath she started to unwrap it, although she had a pretty good idea what was in it. She didn't have to unwrap it completely before she could see it was several layers of plastic bags around white powder. She rewrapped the packet and put it carefully away in her purse before she washed her hands thoroughly. She needed to go home. She needed time to think.

As she walked through the diner towards the front door, the waitress called, "Thank you, Honey. Have a nice day."

June smiled and waved without slowing down. It probably wouldn't be a nice day.

June rushed into her apartment at 7:30 am. She felt massively relieved. She had experienced a major attack of paranoia on the bus when she was sure someone was following her. He got off the bus and June realized she was just imagining things. She was so freaked out she missed her usual stop and had to get off at the next one and walk the three blocks back to her building.

She didn't have a clue what she should do. She couldn't believe the mess she had managed to get into.

Alright, she thought, *let's try and think rationally.*

The first thing she needed to do, was to decide whether or not she should go into work like it was just a normal day. Because it was just a normal day. BECAUSE IT WAS JUST A NORMAL DAY.

June turned on her TV and put on the morning news. The weather guy was on. June tried to listen, but she couldn't think. She sighed and took the packet out of her purse. She opened it flat on the coffee table and removed the outer bags. The lumpy white powder was obviously coke, but June stuck her finger in the bag and tasted a tiny speck. It was good to be positive, she decided.

She held the bag in one hand, testing its weight. She hadn't the faintest idea how much she was holding, but it seemed like a lot to her. She figured it was worth a LOT of money, and she was in big trouble. She couldn't go to the police. She couldn't risk all her friends and their circumstances just because of Jerry and Chip.

Maybe she wasn't in trouble after all. Nobody knew she had taken it. It wouldn't be missed for a couple of days. When the frantic call came from Oshkosh, they would wonder if they put the packet in the wrong box.

In spite of everything, June smiled. It might not put Chip out of business, but it would cripple them for a bit, and maybe make them rethink things.

June stared at the bag, and for a second she thought about keeping it. Maybe she should keep a little, or at least try it.

That is the trouble with coke.

She laughed at herself and took the bag into her bathroom. She only paused for a second, and then dumped the lot into the toilet. She flushed a couple of times and rinsed out the bags in the sink and threw everything away, burying it under some trash.

She looked at herself in the mirror. She looked like crap. Her mascara had smeared all around her eyes and it made her look like a raccoon with a hangover. She stripped off and took a quick shower. All she had to do now was to act as if nothing had happened. She threw on a sweatshirt and jeans and was out the door in time to catch her usual bus.

As she rode to work, she decided she felt a lot better than she expected, considering the circumstances. She felt…happy. Almost.

June came into the outer office with a cheery, "Good morning."

"Yeah," Debbie grunted. Debbie looked like shit. June tried not to laugh at her.

Just then, Jerry came out of his office. "Hello, June," he boomed.

"Good morning, Jerry," June smiled at him.

"What's wrong?" Jerry suddenly looked at June with concern, causing June to practically jump out of her Nikes. "Do you feel alright?"

"Well, to be honest, I'm a little hung over," June smiled nervously.

"Really? So is Debbie," he said loudly in Debbie's direction. "Aren't you, dear?"

Debbie scowled at Jerry.

"I always know when something is wrong. I could tell by your eyes," Jerry claimed.

June tittered, "That's very good, Jerry. You're very observant."

"I know," Jerry crowed. "I'll tell you another thing, too. You were out last night with Ann, weren't you?"

"Um…" June stalled.

"You can't get anything past me. I know because Ann called in sick this morning, and you always go out together," Jerry said triumphantly.

"You got us, Jerry," June admitted. "You sure are a sharp one."

"By the way," Jerry snapped his fingers. "Remind me to get you a new key for the phone room. I'm having Virgil replace the lock."

"Oh, good," June lied. "It's been sticky or something."

June went to her desk and straightened out everything from the night before. Ann and Thor must have hit it off well if she called in sick. Or maybe she really was so hungover she couldn't make it into work.

June decided to ask the packing room ladies if they had a couple of aspirin.

CHAPTER 15

MONDAY, NOVEMBER 14, 1988

Tensions were running high at Rock Shirt. Most of the employees had no idea about the cause of the tension, but everyone could feel it. They had all heard about the arguments that had taken place in Jerry's office even if they hadn't heard the screaming personally.

Monday and Tuesday of the previous week had been very quiet. It took a couple of days for June's theft to be noticed. On Wednesday something must have happened. June figured the call had come from Oshkosh, and that's when the screaming started.

June heard the commotion all the way in the phone room. She heard Jerry yelling first. It was a one-sided conversation, so June surmised Jerry was arguing with someone over the phone.

She got up and headed down the hall toward Jerry's

office. She hung back in the hall, but she wanted to get close enough to hear the gist of the conversation.

"WE DID," Jerry insisted loudly. "I was THERE. I saw it."

There was a short pause before Jerry resumed, "You are trying to BULLSHIT ME. It HAS to be there."

After another pause, Jerry slammed down the phone and blasted, "DEBBIE, get in here."

The heavy oak door slammed, and June could hear the muffled voices of Debbie and Jerry screaming. They were trying to scream over each other, and June crept a little closer to try to make out what they were saying.

She definitely heard Debbie scream the word, "LIAR," more than once. It was very ugly, and June felt a little panicky, even though nobody suspected her having a part in the mystery

June thought it best to stay out of the way. She hurried back to her desk. She sincerely hoped they were freaked out enough to call off whatever shit Chip had talked Jerry into.

She hoped Jerry had sense enough to feel the Feds breathing down his neck.

Sales were slow for a Monday. Phone people were sitting around and talking over coffee. June was already on edge when the intercom on her desk buzzed, making her jump three inches out of her seat. Despite its tonal similarity to an alarm clock, the intercom was one of Virgil's most helpful creations. June rarely saw Virgil, but evidence of his work was unmistakable.

June hit the button on the intercom. "Hello. This is the phone room."

It was Jerry, but it sounded like he had his intercom

completely inside of his mouth. "It's a bust. The Feds are here again..." June made out the word 'Feds' and leapt to her feet.

June shouted, "BUST!"

As usual, there was a lot of noise and commotion, and the reaction of the room was mixed. She whistled a short blast before continuing. "Take what you can carry and run. NOW!"

They had covered what to do if they were busted, so this time people knew how to react. June handed the pile of orders from her desk to Sharon on the way out and told her to shove them down her pants. Sharon did, and then tried to waddle stiffly down the hall.

One of the agents tried to stop Sharon from leaving. "Don't go just yet, Miss. We need to talk to you."

"I need to be sick," Sharon blurted out. June was surprised that Sharon was such a good actress, but maybe she really needed to throw up.

The agent decided not to take a chance and let her pass. June tried to go with her, but the agent blocked her way. She thought she recognized him from last time, and from the look he was giving June, she guessed he recognized her, too. "I can't let you leave until you give us some information."

"I don't have any information to give you," June said more calmly than she felt. "Anyway, I'm not leaving. I just want to go into the office and talk with Jerry."

"We'll go together." He held the door open for June. She did NOT like the way he said that.

She gave him a weak smile and walked into Jerry's office. She realized things were much worse than the last time. Several agents were tearing the place apart. This time they were not being considerate or careful. Several of the plants were dumped upside down on the rug. One agent had Jerry in the back corner of the room, and he was asking him questions. Jerry was refusing to answer them without his lawyer.

Debbie was gone, so June assumed she had gotten out with the books. Jerry would make sure the records got out before he worried about anything else.

Jerry saw June as she entered the office. "Ah, there you are, Sam," he said to June.

June tried not to smirk.

"I have been calling my lawyer, but his line is busy. These gentlemen refuse to wait. They are tearing apart my office and ruining my business." He gave his lines like a Shakespearian actor.

"We have a WARRANT, Mr. Cooper," the agent questioning Jerry said.

Jerry handed his car keys to June. "Go and get the lawyer."

The agent with June shook his head. "She can't leave until she answers some questions."

"She isn't anybody. She's my cleaning lady," Jerry lied. "You don't need to talk to her. I need my lawyer. She will bring him right back. It's my constitutional right to have a lawyer."

The agent took the car keys. "I need to see some identification," he said too loudly.

"I don't have any," June lied.

"Then you can't drive a car without a license."

June hadn't thought of that.

"We have all the records. It shouldn't be too hard for us to figure out who you are. Of course, going through it all will take some time. You could speed things up by cooperating."

"I told you, I don't have any ID." June's purse was locked in the bottom drawer of her desk.

"We will have to take you in until we can identify you," he threatened.

"You can't arrest me," June protested. She looked around frantically for an escape route but there were too many agents in the room, including one blocking the door.

"I certainly can," the agent stepped closer.

"You don't have to say anything until the lawyer gets here," Jerry argued.

June was scared. If she was sure about anything, she was sure she needed a lawyer. She decided it was for the best to keep her mouth shut.

June's agent, whose name plate said 'PITTER,' kept asking her the same questions over and over again.

"What is your name? What job do you do here? How long have you worked for Mr. Cooper?"

June just stood looking at Jerry with her mouth clamped shut. Agent Pitter eventually grew bored with her silence and gave her a choice.

"If you don't agree to answer a few simple questions, I will have no choice but to take you in!"

June shook her head. Jerry looked pleased.

Pitter took a pair of handcuffs off his belt and Jerry stopped looking pleased. June looked panicky.

Pitter handcuffed her and spouted all the legal stuff they have to tell you when they arrest you. June wasn't listening to him; she was listening to Jerry.

"I'll take care of everything. The lawyer will have you out in no time. I'll even pay for it and everything." Jerry assured her.

June wanted to smack Jerry, but unfortunately her hands were cuffed behind her back. She had to settle for giving him an acidic glare as she was led out.

Pitter took her down in the elevator and locked her in the back of one of the blue vans. To June, it felt like he left her there for an eternity. She was scared. It was cold, and June didn't have a coat, and the back of the van smelled like dirty feet.

Eventually she heard a lot of voices, and somebody started the van. She couldn't see who it was or where she was going. When the van stopped, Pitter opened the back and helped June out. She was at the downtown jail on State Street.

Pitter gave it one more shot. "I have to take you in and turn you over to the Milwaukee County Sheriff's Department. Once I sign you over to them, they will be responsible for getting you to cooperate. If you agree to answer my questions, I can take your statement over at the Federal Building and you won't be taken into custody. If I take you into the jail, they WILL book you. You really don't want that to happen, do you?"

June started to cry. She didn't know what to do. She didn't trust Pitter and she didn't want to talk to him without the lawyer being present. She didn't want to get arrested, obviously, but she thought she might be better off dealing with someone else without Pitter being there.

Keeping her mouth shut was the only decision she had been able to come to so far, and she stubbornly decided to stick with the plan.

"Very well," Pitter sighed, and led June into the huge white building. June hoped she would make Pitter do a lot of extra paperwork. He nodded to the officer on the front desk and led June to the elevators.

He took her to the second floor, and as they got out she saw a sign that said Prisoner Processing. It was a large room with rows of seats like they had at the airport.

There were about a dozen people in the room, mostly men, watching a little TV bolted near the ceiling. They all watched with interest when June was brought in. They were all there on assorted charges by the Milwaukee Police. It wasn't often that someone was brought in by the Feds.

They all watched as Pitter led June through the waiting area and into a long narrow room that reminded June of the Milwaukee County Zoo. It was all white tiled, and it had a long bench along one wall, which was also tiled. There were baggies tossed on the bench that looked like they contained two slices of white bread with a slice of bologna in between. Every couple feet along the wall was a ring that was bolted into the wall. There were two men handcuffed to rings and sitting on the bench when June was brought in. One of them was trying to eat a sandwich while handcuffed.

June's stomach flipped over. The room had a zooish smell to it and June wanted to change her mind, but she was more afraid of Pitter than the Milwaukee jail. She'd be out in no time, she reasoned.

Pitter took her to the far end of the bench and handcuffed her to one of the rings on the wall "Just sit here. Eat a sandwich if you want." He walked out the way they had come in.

"Hey, baby," one of the men across the room leaned way over so he could look at June. "Whatcha in for, trickin'?"

June mortified herself further by starting to cry again. She was VERY scared, and she wished she could think of a way to extract herself from the mess she was in.

She cursed Jerry and the day she met him. She cursed

herself for being stupid enough for taking a job at Rock Shirt in the first place. She wondered what her mother would think if she could see her now.

A woman came into the room and sat next to June on the bench. She had a clipboard and a name tag that said 'UERCHT.' June wondered how it was pronounced.

"Hello. I'm a nurse. I need to ask you a few questions before we accept you into custody. Do you understand?"

"Yes," June said weakly.

"What is your name?"

There was a short pause before she answered, "June." She tried to stop crying but failed.

"Okay, June," the nurse said gently, "Do you feel alright?"

"I guess so," June said as she tried to find a more comfortable position on the bench.

"Do you have any health problems? Are you on any medication? Do you use street drugs?"

"No," June answered a lengthy list of health-related questions.

"Last question," the woman said. "What is your last name?"

"Forrest."

"Okay, wait here." The woman got up and left.

"Where does she think I'm going to go?" June said to herself, making the two men across the room laugh.

June summoned up the courage to look directly at them for the first time. They were young and black, VERY young, June realized. The closest man to her was slightly above average height and heavy. The man further away was only about 5'3'', and skinny. He had to lean way forward to see past the big man.

"June," the skinny man said. "You want to tell us what

you're in for?"

"You tell me what you did first," June answered.

"I didn't do nothin'," he said. "I'm innocent." He tried to look angelic.

June laughed. "I think all I did was refuse to cooperate," June wondered. "That better be all, or I'm in worse trouble than I thought."

"Not cooperating with the Feds is bad enough," The fat man said with a chuckle.

"Take my advice and start cooperating," the skinny man said. "If you don't cooperate around here they hurt you."

Just then, a door at the back opened and a deafening din of barking dogs echoed around the tiled space. The two men on the bench looked terrified, pulled up their feet and tried to press themselves into the wall.

A man and a woman wearing Milwaukee County Sheriff uniforms brought two huge German Shepherds on leashes through the room. The noise was unreal. June felt panic rising in her throat, and she wanted to scream but she couldn't. She was frozen with fear.

The woman cop struggled fiercely against the strain of the leash. She noticed the panic-stricken June and said to her, "They were just practicing their attacks. They're a little worked up."

The hustled the dogs out of the room, but it took a long time before June's pulse returned to normal.

A cop came in and took the skinny man out. Several minutes later, another cop collected his friend. June sat where she was for another hour by herself. June decided that jail was very horrible.

What if Jerry couldn't get a hold of the lawyer? What if he was out of town or something? Or out of the country?

Finally, a cop came over to June and unhooked her from the wall. His name badge said 'SCHULTZ.'

"We thought Pitter might change his mind about having you booked, but he said he didn't have time to deal with you right now. He's got a hot date tonight, or something. Guess you're not doing anything, hey?"

He laughed as he led her into a closet sized room with a metal detector in it, like the ones at the airport. He took her handcuffs off and told her to empty her pockets into a plastic bin.

Her pockets contained a Bic lighter, a five, a single, and a handful of change. Her bra contained a joint, but she didn't tell them about that. Fortunately, pot isn't metallic, and neither was her bra. She walked through the detector without a beep. Schultz carried the bin and led her back to the waiting area she had seen as she was brought in.

June was handed over to a woman cop for booking. "I'm Deputy Russell. I am required by law to take your fingerprints and photograph you for the purposes of identification. If you behave yourself, we won't have to lock you up in a little cell or take away any of your privileges. Do you understand?"

"Yes, ma'am." June just wanted to get through this as quickly and quietly as possible.

She had mug shots taken, and then they took her prints. She was surprised they didn't use ink. The deputy rolled her finger on a device like a computer touchpad. She then had to answer all kinds of questions that she had been avoiding in the first place, questions about Rock Shirt, Jerry, and her involvement in the business.

She was then told she could wait in the pen. A couple of rows on the far right were designated as the women's area, and there was a payphone close by, so June went and sat on the end of the row of seats so she could keep an eye on the phone. Once it was free, she could grab it. There were more people in the pen than when she first arrived, probably two dozen, and some of them didn't look very nice.

"June," someone called her name. She turned around and saw the two men she had met earlier. June moved back a row so she could sit closer to them.

"What are your names?" June asked.

"My name is Andrew," the fat man said, "and this is Marcus.

"Nice to meet you," June said, trying to keep one eye on the phone. "Can you tell me when that woman hangs up?" she asked them.

"Why are you in trouble with the Feds?" Andrew persisted.

June sighed, "I guess you could call it copyright infringement."

"What's that?" Marcus asked.

"I work for a bootleg t-shirt company," June said as quietly as she could.

They laughed. "Is that all? We could tell you never been in jail before."

"So, what did you do?" June asked.

"I told you, nothin'," Marcus insisted.

"Okay, what do they SAY you did."

"Burglary, man," Marcus said sadly.

"I just violated my parole," Andrew said.

"How'd you do that?" Marcus asked him.

"Failed my drug test, AGAIN."

Marcus pointed at the phone. "It's free now."

June jumped out of her seat and ran over to the phone. She called Jerry collect, since they had taken her money.

She was relieved when he answered and accepted the charges.

"Jerry," June yelled too loudly. "I'm in JAIL, Jerry. You've got to get me out of here."

"I know, I know," Jerry said. "Monty is down there now. He is trying to get you out at this very minute."

"How long will it take?"

"I don't know. Not long. Hang in there. Everything that can be done, is being done."

June heard someone giggling in the background. There were a lot of suspicious noises, June realized.

"What's going on there, Jerry?"

"Nothing at all. I'm working late, trying to clean up the mess in here."

"You had better take care of this, Jerry." June was starting to panic again.

"Don't worry."

June hung up. She was very, VERY, worried.

Monty finally came for June late that night. June was wishing she had eaten a bologna sandwich when she had the chance.

While Monty drove her home, he told her that he thought they would probably drop the charges against her. She had only been arrested because she didn't cooperate. No one else was charged.

When June got home, she made herself a can of soup and went to bed. As she started to doze off, she told herself that tomorrow she was definitely taking a day off work and buying a car

CHAPTER 17

FRIDAY, DECEMBER 16, 1988

During the next few weeks, June bought a nice used car, found a nice new job, and Rock Shirt was raided three more times. The car was nothing to look at, but it was a low milage Malibu with excellent maintenance records.

The new job was for a management position—managing an office of data entry workers. The pay was unexciting, but they offered great benefits. She would be starting at her new job right after the first of the year.

The series of raids were bad, and they lost most of their bestselling shirts. Once one management company had found them, it was easy for the rest of them to pile on. They lost a lot of employees, most of the newer ones. The same old crew was prepared to ride out the storm, but June wanted out. It had stopped being fun a long time ago.

Also, reporters were hanging around all the time so there was no avoiding them. June wrapped a winter scarf around her face and hurried past with a muttered, "No comment" so often it was absurd.

Her mother had seen the news reports and freaked out. Fortunately, June was able to tell her mother she had given notice and would be leaving Rock Shirt for a more stable job. She still hadn't told her mother about the day she spent in jail.

Jerry had tried to talk June out of leaving when she gave him her notice. He agreed to give her a good reference and had in fact gone completely overboard. When her new boss had called him, he made June sound like a cross between Princess Diana and Mother Teresa.

But now it was June's last day. To celebrate, Jerry threw a big party in the phone room. The Popping Cherries played, and nobody got any work done.

The phone room that on June's first day had seemed huge and empty, was now packed to overflowing. Jerry had invited everyone. A lot of former employees were there, and people from other businesses in the building started crashing the party once the band started playing.

June was having a great time. She was checking out the buffet table when Jerry put his arm around her shoulders.

The band finished a set to thunderous applause. "Are you having fun?" Jerry asked her once the noise had died down.

"This is a GREAT party, Jerry. Thanks."

"Don't leave," he said suddenly. "My plants will die."

"I have to, Jerry."

"Did I tell you Leo is coming back?"

"That's not funny."

"I'm not kidding! He'll be here any minute."

"Did you talk him into coming back because you

thought it might make me change my mind about leaving?"

"Does it?" Jerry raised an eyebrow.

"No."

"We'll see. What would I do without you?"

"What ARE you going to do, Jerry? Are you going to promote somebody or advertise for a new person?"

"Debbie wants the job."

"Why does she want to be the sales manager?"

"Why else? She wants the commission."

"And you're just going to give it to her?"

"Yes."

June looked Jerry straight in the eyes. "What has she got on you, Jerry?"

A lightning bolt of terror darted across Jerry's face and was gone. "I don't know what you mean?"

"Jerry, why does she keep the books when she hasn't even graduated high school? Why does she follow you around like a smirking shadow? Why do you give in to her whenever she asks for something?"

He put on his insincere 'working smile' and shook June's hand. "It's been great working with you. Don't be a stranger. Visit us anytime." He patted her head and went to join the party people.

As she watched him go, she knew he was as done with her as she was with him.

"Hello," said an unmistakable voice behind her.

"Hello, Leo." June turned around and for a moment, forgot about everything else.

"I heard you was leavin'," he said quietly, or as quietly as he could with all the noise in the room.

June just nodded, not trusting her voice.

"Good."

June hiccupped, because she didn't know whether to laugh or cry.

"I knew you'd get wise sooner or later." Leo said.

"You mean...you're not coming back to work for Jerry?"

"Hell no, I only come to see you." He grinned broadly as June stood blinking at him.

"Me?"

Leo laughed. "Who is dis party for? I hope you're not mad at me for staying away."

"No, of course not," June said. "How have you been?"

"I been better, but I got a lawyer now, and he's going to try to get me legal right quick. Him thinks I can stay for good, but I got to stay out of trouble! Dat's why I was keeping shy of Jerry."

"It's been pretty hot around here," June agreed. "But they haven't come after any of the employees."

"Except for you?"

"So....you heard about that."

"I heard dey trew you in da jailhouse," Leo teased.

"Only for the day. It was kind of my own fault."

"No it weren't," Leo laughed. "You would never cause trouble."

"Well, I was working here, and that was trouble enough."

"Why did you stay here for so long? You never told me your 'circumstances.'"

June had been thinking about that a lot. It was hard for her to look at her own faults objectively, although she was trying. "I was really broke when I started here. I guess you could call it an act of financial desperation."

"Are you STILL trying to tell me you done it for d'money?" Leo asked with exasperation.

"No. I think I took the job as an act of deliberate irresponsibility. My life was crap, and I didn't know how to fix it. Out of frustration, I threw a monkey wrench in the works."

"Did it work?"

"In a way. It certainly changed me, I hope for the better. I don't think I will ever regret it, in spite of everything."

"Good. If you never worked here, I never would have met you." Leo smiled broadly at June. "Dat, I would regret."

"Hey, guess what?" June was suddenly excited. "I'm not your boss anymore."

Leo looked perplexed, and June laughed. She kissed him and laughed at his surprised expression. Leo kissed her back so suddenly, June nearly toppled over backwards. They laughed and hung onto each other for so long, people started throwing hors d'oeuvres at them.

Maybe the t-shirts were lying all the time. Maybe life wasn't a bitch after all.

ABOUT THE AUTHOR

Mary Denomie is a retired librarian from Wisconsin.
She has a rescue cat and likes to crochet a LOT.
Bootleg Shirt is her first novel.
Follow Mary on Twitter @MaryDenomie